## AMBUSHING THE AMBUSHERS

Slocum cocked the lever action, jacking another cartridge into the firing chamber as the empty brass hull ejected. He swung the Winchester barrel to bear on another man a few yards away from the one he had shot and caught him in his sights. The man looked up and started to point, but his arm never got high enough. Slocum squeezed the trigger and saw blood blossom in the center of the man's chest as the 180 grain projectile slammed into his breastbone. Blood and bone sprayed out of the man's back, and he crumpled like a wad of dirty laundry.

Two other men saw Slocum and they swung their rifles in his direction. One of them was in the open and Slocum levered another shell into the chamber and sighted quickly on the man's throat. He fired. Fragments of rock splashed from a spot near his head, but he saw his target go down, his throat torn to shreds.

# DON'T MISS THESE
## ALL-ACTION WESTERN SERIES
## FROM THE BERKLEY PUBLISHING GROUP

### THE GUNSMITH by J. R. Roberts

Clint Adams was a legend among lawmen, outlaws, and ladies. They called him . . . the Gunsmith.

### LONGARM by Tabor Evans

The popular long-running series about Deputy U.S. Marshal Long—his life, his loves, his fight for justice.

### SLOCUM by Jake Logan

Today's longest-running action Western. John Slocum rides a deadly trail of hot blood and cold steel.

### BUSHWHACKERS by B. J. Lanagan

An action-packed series by the creators of Longarm! The rousing adventures of the most brutal gang of cutthroats ever assembled—Quantrill's Raiders.

### DIAMONDBACK by Guy Brewer

Dex Yancey is Diamondback, a Southern gentleman turned con man when his brother cheats him out of the family fortune. Ladies love him. Gamblers hate him. But nobody pulls one over on Dex. . . .

### WILDGUN by Jack Hanson

The blazing adventures of mountain man Will Barlow—from the creators of Longarm!

### TEXAS TRACKER by Tom Calhoun

Meet J.T. Law: the most relentless—and dangerous—manhunter in all Texas. Where sheriffs and posses fail, he's the best man to bring in the most vicious outlaws—for a price.

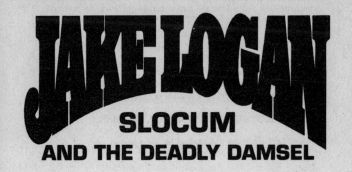

# JAKE LOGAN

## SLOCUM
# AND THE DEADLY DAMSEL

JOVE BOOKS, NEW YORK

SLOCUM AND THE DEADLY DAMSEL

A Jove Book / published by arrangement with
the author

PRINTING HISTORY
Jove edition / August 2003

For information address: The Berkley Publishing Group,
a division of Penguin Group (USA) Inc.,
375 Hudson Street, New York, New York 10014.

ISBN: 0-515-13584-4

A JOVE BOOK®
Jove Books are published by The Berkley Publishing Group,
a division of Penguin Group (USA) Inc.,
375 Hudson Street, New York, New York 10014.
JOVE and the "J" design
are trademarks belonging to Penguin Group (USA) Inc.

PRINTED IN THE UNITED STATES OF AMERICA

10   9   8   7   6   5   4   3   2   1

# 1

John Slocum wanted to frown, but he didn't. He didn't
like the deal much, but he had learned a long time ago
never to let his feelings show on his face. That way, nobody could take advantage of him, nor see the hand he
was holding.

"I figger you like that Palousa so damned much, you'll
go through hell and high water to get him back, Slocum."

"When I make a promise to a man, Biggers, I keep it."

Logan Biggers was a small man, not only in stature,
but in mind. He stood well beneath Slocum's shoulders,
and his bulbous face was damp with a sheen of sweat.
Slocum knew Biggers was nervous. And worried. But,
still, he didn't like the way the man did business.

Biggers ran a pretty big stable and feedstore just on the
edge of Pueblo. He said his wisdom had guided him to
build where he did before the town was destroyed some
years before, and now he was thriving. He provided
horses, cattle, and sometimes sheep, to ranchers in the
Rocky Mountains. Slocum figured him to be more of a

broker than a stableman. In fact, Biggers had been re-
ferred to him by a rancher to whom Slocum had delivered
a herd of horses he drove to Jefferson Territory from Mis-
souri.

"That's a good deal of money I'm entrusting to you,
Slocum, and for all I know, you could just pocket it and
light a shuck. I need those horses out of Santa Fe real
bad."

"And, I said I'd pick them up for you and drive 'em
back here to Pueblo."

"I know, and you come with good bona fides, Slocum,
but a man's got to be real careful these days."

"I'm as careful as the next man, and I don't go back
on a promise, as I told you."

"Well, just in case, I know you put great store in that
Palousa, and I'd feel better about holding him as a kind
of secure deposit until you bring back those horses."

"I don't like much letting a stranger take care of that
horse, Biggers."

"I'll take real good care of him. You've seen the way
I treat my stock."

Slocum had to admit that Biggers was not a sloppy
stableman. It was obvious that he took care of the
horseflesh in his care. There probably was no real reason
to worry.

"I grant you that," Slocum said.

"Fine. You can ride that black gelding. He's a four-
year-old, with good bottom, good lungs, sturdy legs. He's
a better horse for where you're going. He's got Arab
blood in him."

"I noticed the small feet," Slocum said. "He looks to
be a good horse."

"He'll come to your whistle, and he won't give out on you."

"Fine. If those are the conditions, I guess I'll do the job for you."

"Who was it sent you to me again?" Biggers asked.

"A man named Ford, lives up the canyon."

"Fargo Ford?"

"That's the man. I delivered a dozen Missouri-bred horses to him yesterday."

"Ford's a good man. I reckon if he can trust you, so can I."

"But only so far," Slocum said.

Biggers didn't smile. "I got to watch out for my interests," he said.

"You take good care of that Palousa, Biggers, or you and I will tangle."

"I reckon that's fair enough, Slocum. Have you ever ridden to Santa Fe before?"

"I've been there."

"From here?"

"No, but I know the way well enough."

"The way ain't all it is, Slocum."

"Oh? What else?"

"That's still a very dangerous trail. You've got a pass to go over and there are renegades, Injuns, and road agents just looking for a ripe pilgrim like yourself."

"You think I'm a pilgrim?"

"Well, I didn't mean no offense, but you're green on this here trail, I reckon, and they's some what will be lookin' for such as you."

"I'll keep my eyes peeled. But if you haven't told anyone about me, and I sure as hell haven't, then nobody should know I'm packing your cash. Right, Biggers?"

"Right. I don't talk my business in town or anywheres else."

"Then I'll just be a man riding the trail to Santa Fe."

"They was a party lit out this morning. You might run into them. Don't know much about them, but they seemed all right. Kind of secretive and all, but honest enough. They bought a couple of horses from me yesterday, picked 'em up this mornin'."

"I'll keep an eye out for them, too," Slocum said.

"They go by the name of Travers. They're goin' slow, so you'll likely catch up to them along the way. But, was I you, I'd keep on riding. You just never know who you can trust."

"I gather you don't trust many folks," Slocum said.

"In my business, you got to be right on top of things."

"I'm sure."

Slocum saddled the black gelding, gave the Palousa a good-bye pat and started off. Biggers waved to him, but Slocum didn't wave back. He was glad to be away from the man. But his money was as good as anyone's and Biggers was paying a fair price for a long ride to Santa Fe and a long drive back with twenty horses. Slocum was to meet a man in Santa Fe named Paco Delgado, who would ride back with him, help with the herd.

Slocum had grub enough to last him until he got to Taos, where he would reprovision before making the last leg to Santa Fe. He was well armed and confident that he could handle any difficulty along the way, with road agents or Indians. As long as he kept his head.

The rugged backbone of the Rocky Mountains stood jagged and snowcapped against the western sky as Slocum rode south on the plain. He knew that this had once been a dangerous road, but that was before his time, when

Ute and Arapaho roamed the mountains and plains, when the Southern Cheyenne and Comanche and Paiutes came in war parties to raid other bands of Indians and the settlements. But he had heard that after the War of Secession, the country had tamed down some. Of course, he knew there were always those who refused to give up their former lives and lived as they always had, before civilization began its creep from East to West.

He could see for miles, and while he kept his eye on the foothills for signs of other humans with criminal intentions, he also gazed often at the long prairie that was dotted with buttes and mesas and rocky spires. The horse rode well under him, and he was satisfied that Biggers had not given him a bad one.

The road began to rise gradually, and the way ahead was now rimmed with rocky outcroppings on either side as he headed for the high pass they called Rabbit Ears.

He knew the horse was eating up miles and it showed no signs of tiring even when the afternoon shadows began to lengthen and stripe the road ahead.

Slocum was just beginning to relax when he heard the crackle of rifle fire.

The horse balked and its ears turned to twisting cones as it listened and tried to pinpoint where the sound was coming from.

"Easy, boy," Slocum said, patting the gelding's neck. At the same time, he slipped his '73 Winchester .44 from its sheath and lay it across the pommel of his saddle.

More gunfire, and it was coming from someplace up ahead. And, it was close. Slocum left the road then and rode toward an outcropping of rock on high ground.

He circled the rocks carefully and came to a halt when he saw the wagon stopped in the middle of the road. He saw flashes of orange flame as men on horseback shot toward the wagon, and he heard a couple of shots coming from the wagon.

Then he heard a man scream in agony, and the sound sent shivers up Slocum's back.

One of the men by the wagon rose up and staggered forward, clutching his chest. And there was blood spewing from a bullet hole just below his rib cage.

Slocum only saw one other man, and he knew that if he didn't act fast, that man, too, would soon be dead.

Slocum lifted his rifle and jacked a cartridge into the chamber. A thought crossed his mind that he was about to even the odds.

**2**

Slocum counted at least five men surrounding the wagon. All of them were shooting at a lone man who seemed to be the only survivor of the wagon. It didn't take much figuring to know that the lone man was in deep trouble, and unless he got help, he would soon join the other man who lay on the ground, stiff as a board.

Slocum moved close to the rock outcropping and picked a target, a man with a rifle who was lying prone, firing at the besieged man near the wagon. Slocum leveled the front blade sight on the man's back, lined it up with the buckhorn rear sight and centered his aim just between the man's shoulder blades. He held his breath and squeezed the trigger. The rifle cracked and bucked against his shoulder with the force of its recoil. He saw the man twitch and try to rise, but the rifle fell from his hands, and he lay still, flat against the ground.

Slocum cocked the lever action, jacking another cartridge into the firing chamber as the empty brass hull ejected. He swung the Winchester barrel to bear on another man a few yards away from the one he had shot and caught him in his sights. The man looked up and started to point, but his arm never got high enough. Slocum squeezed the trigger and saw blood blossom in the center of the man's chest as the 180 grain projectile slammed into his breastbone. Blood and bone sprayed out of the man's back, and he crumpled like a wad of dirty laundry.

Two other men saw Slocum, and they swung their rifles in his direction. One of them was in the open, and Slocum levered another shell into the chamber and sighted quickly on the man's throat. He fired and ducked as he heard a rifle boom. Fragments of rock splashed from a spot near his head, but he saw his target go down, his throat torn to shreds.

Then, he saw another man rise up from behind some brush and yell at the one Slocum planned to shoot next.

"Let's get the hell out of here, Clyde."

Clyde, if that was his name, turned quickly and fired one last shot, not at Slocum, but at the man hiding near the wagon. Slocum saw that man twist in pain and stagger a few feet before he fell on his side. He was reaching for his leg.

Slocum slammed another bullet into the chamber and swung on Clyde, but the man scrambled like a land crab and disappeared over a hump of land.

Slocum waited, but he saw no more bushwhackers. A few moments later, he heard the sound of hoofbeats and when he stood up in the stirrups, he saw two men riding south at a ground-eating gallop. One of the men turned to look back, and his hat blew off his head. The hat was held by a thong around the neck.

Just for the hell of it, Slocum sent a last round in their

direction and heard the bullet whine as it spanged off a rock near Clyde, who ducked and started kicking his horse and slapping his reins on the animal's rump.

"Hello the wagon," Slocum called.

"Help," he heard in reply.

"I'll be right down. How many men did you count?"

"F-five," the man said, and his voice was quavery and weak.

"Hold on," Slocum said. He slid three more cartridges in the chamber of his rifle and headed down from the hillock toward the wagon. There were two horses hitched to it, and another tied to the rear. The wagon was covered, which was unusual, he thought, and from the tracks, seemed to be carrying a heavy load. Slocum wondered what the cargo was.

"Mister, I hope you're on my side," the man said when Slocum rode up. "Otherwise, I've got a bead on you, and I'll blow you right out your saddle."

"Hold on, son," Slocum said. "I'm the one who shot three of those jaspers who were bent on putting your lamp out."

"I'm hit," the man said. "In the leg, I think."

"Hold on," Slocum said. "I'll take a gander."

The man was dressed in heavy duck pants and a chambray shirt of faded blue. He lay on his side next to the wagon tongue, a rifle in his hands, his one leg drenched in blood below the knee.

"You can put away that rifle," Slocum said. "What's your name?"

"Benjamin Travers. Call me Ben. Who are you?"

"I'm John Slocum. Biggers told me I might run into you."

"Biggers. He might have been the one who set those men on us."

"I doubt it. I think Biggers, for all his faults, shoots pretty straight."

"Well, they come at us out of nowhere, like a pack of wild dogs. We didn't have a chance. Like they was waiting for us."

Slocum looked around. From his vantage point next to the wagon he could see why a band of road agents might pick that spot. The ground was covered with horse tracks and human footprints, some new, some old. All this Slocum noticed at a glance and with a quick, practiced scan.

"This is a perfect place for an ambush," Slocum said. "And from the looks of all these tracks, you're not the first pilgrim to be waylaid here by brigands."

"I'm mighty suspicious, just the same."

"Who's that on the ground yonder?" Slocum asked. "He looks to be dead."

"That's my pa," Travers said, and he squeezed his eyes shut as tears burst from them in a flood.

"Sorry."

"He got shot right off. In the heart. I couldn't save him. He was gone by the time I got to him."

"Well, let's take a look at that leg of yours," Slocum said, climbing out of the saddle. He tied the black gelding to the rear wagon wheel and walked over to the young man. He squatted down and pulled away the torn pant leg to view the wound. Slocum let out a slow whistle.

"Bad?" Travers asked.

"I don't know yet. I'll have to cut away some of your pants cloth there and wash the wound for a better look."

"It hurts like fire."

"I expect it does, Travers. You've got a slug in your leg. It didn't come out the other side."

"It feels like the bone is broken."

Slocum looked at the entry wound, gently touched the back of the leg. He didn't feel any bone splinters.

"You're lucky in one way, Travers. The lead hit you in the calf, which is mostly flesh. I don't think it struck a bone. But that lead's got to come out. Even so, you might lose that leg. At least from just below the knee on down."

"You mean I might wind up as a peg leg?"

"Better some wood on your leg than in a cross over your grave."

"Damn," Travers swore.

"That bullet might have nicked an artery. There's a hell of a lot of blood. Too much for a flesh wound. I'm going to take that bandanna from around your neck and make a tourniquet above the wound. You're still leaking blood, and when I move you, you could bleed out."

"Bleed out?"

"Lose so much blood you'd probably die right on the spot."

Travers swore again.

"Let me find a stick or something, and then you'll have to keep it tight and loosen it every few minutes."

"What do you mean?" Travers asked.

Slocum found a small stick and removed the bandanna from around Travers's neck. With his big knife, he slit the trouser leg and exposed the wound in Travers's calf. He pulled the cloth up out of the way and rolled the bandanna into a tight rope-like piece. Then he wrapped the tourniquet around the leg just below the knee, placed the stick inside a loop, which he then tied tightly. Then he twisted the stick. He could see the blood stop leaking from the wound.

"That hurts like Billy hell," Travers said.

"But, it stopped the bleeding. You can't leave it so tight like that, so loosen it in about five minutes or so. Then, when it starts to bleed too much, twist that stick until the bleeding stops. Can you do that?"

"Uh huh."

"Your life might depend on it, Travers."

"I can do it."

"Now, let's get you in the shade. I'll build a fire and get to digging out that lead ball. Have you got matches and whiskey?"

"I've got matches in my pocket. I don't have any whiskey."

"Well, I've got both. I hope you like Kentucky straight bourbon, Ben."

"I don't like whiskey of any kind."

"Too bad. I hate to waste good whiskey on someone who doesn't like good Kentucky bourbon."

"Is that where you're from—Kentucky? You have a slight accent."

"Georgia. Calhoun County, but let's get to that leg, son. You watch that tourniquet while I build a fire."

"Slocum, can I trust you?" Travers asked as Slocum rose to his feet.

Slocum looked down at the wounded man. He wondered what was going through Travers's mind at that moment.

"Ben, if you can't trust me, then you're as good as dead."

# 3

Slocum gathered wood for a fire and took the matches from Travers, lit the shavings he had cut to start it. Travers watched in fascination, loosening and tightening the tourniquet around his leg all the while.

"Slocum, I've got to talk to you before you dig that bullet out."

"The sooner I get that bullet out, the better."

"I keep thinking about my father over there. He . . . he's dead, isn't he?"

"Yes, he's dead. I checked him when I was gathering the wood. I'll bury him later."

"I guess I couldn't take him home with me, could I?"

"It wouldn't be a good idea. Not in this heat. You were headed for Taos?"

Travers nodded. "That's where my home is. And I've got to get there. I just hate to bury my father way out here, all alone."

"It won't make any difference to him," Slocum said.

"No, I guess not."

"My sister is waiting for us. I mean, me. We have a home north of Taos, a small ranch."

"You left your sister there, all alone?"

"Yes. That's why I have to know if I can trust you. I have to get there, Slocum. There's something I have to tell her. Something my father was going to do himself."

"It's a long ride to Taos, son," Slocum said.

"I know. You've got to help me get there, Slocum. Please."

"I'm going that way. But what's the urgency? You were not traveling light. With that covered wagon there and the load you're carrying, you made an easy target for highwaymen."

"My sister is older than I am. And she's waiting there. All alone. I-I have to see her as soon as possible."

"Why didn't you just ride on ahead, then? Seems to me you would have had a better chance by yourself."

"I-I have my reasons," Travers said.

"I hope they were good ones," Slocum said as he stirred the fire, added more wood.

Before he started on Ben's leg, he walked to a high point and surveyed the country around. He looked for a long time, but the bushwhackers were nowhere to be seen. Nor could he see anyone else in that vast expanse of earth that surrounded him. He walked back down to the blazing fire, added more wood to it. He saw a kettle hanging from the wagon and a wooden water cask. He filled the kettle, put it on the fire. Then, he drew his knife.

"This is going to hurt, Travers. Do you want a bullet to bite? Or a stick in your mouth?"

"No. I-I can take it, I think."

"Suit yourself. I'll get the whiskey." Slocum laid his knife on a rock next to the fire with just the blade jutting out into the flames. He walked to his horse, dug out a bottle of straight Kentucky bourbon, Old Taylor, and carried it to Ben Travers. He pulled the cork and handed the bottle to the young man.

"Take a long pull on this, Travers."

"It smells strong," Travers said as he sniffed the bottle. Slocum smiled as Travers upended the quart and swallowed a mouthful of whiskey. Travers choked and spluttered, tried to hand the bottle back to Slocum.

"No, you'll need more than that. When I put that hot knife to you, you'll want to jump out of your skin. Take another pull, then take a deep breath and hold it."

Travers swallowed another mouthful, held it down and then drew a deep breath. His eyes watered, but he didn't choke this time.

"You might get to like it," Slocum said.

"Never. It took my breath away."

"Let it smolder in your belly for a minute or two. Then, hold on."

Slocum saw that his knife blade was turning blue and knew it was sterilized. He drew it away from the fire, then walked over to Travers, knelt down and checked the tourniquet.

"I'm going to loosen this for a minute, then tighten it up again. When I get it real tight, I'm going in after that bullet."

"You go right ahead," Travers said, with a slight slur in his voice.

Slocum loosened the tourniquet and watched to see if the blood flowed right back out the hole. He waited several seconds and was glad to see that there was only a slight leaking of fresh blood. Still, he knew that the blood vessels were crimped some from the tight tourniquet and if Travers moved, or tried to stand up, he'd gush blood like a fountain.

Slocum twisted the stick and tightened the tourniquet again. He handed Travers the bottle. "If it hurts too damned much, take another swallow. Try not to think about this knife going inside. It'll only make it worse. The pain, I mean."

"All right," Travers said tightly.

Slocum gingerly put the tip of the knife blade at the wound entrance, then began to shove it through the hole gently, trying to follow the path of the lead slug.

Travers screamed when Slocum's knife penetrated his torn flesh. His body stiffened as if he'd had a steel rod rammed up his spine. He arched his back and then slumped, his head falling on his shoulder as he fell into a dead swoon.

"Good," Slocum muttered, and began to probe for the bullet. He didn't want to tear any arteries up, or make the wound worse, so he went slow, grateful that Travers had passed out.

The bottle in Travers's hand rolled away as his fingers relaxed. Slocum continued probing for the slug, sensitive to any change in pressure at the tip of the knife blade. He felt the blade slide next to a bone and then give way only to strike something hard further on. He pushed gently and felt the object give a little. He withdrew his knife and buried his right index finger inside the wound, pressing hard to go deeper until he felt the bone again. Something pricked his fingertip and he dug at it with his fingernail, felt it come free. He worked the slender sharp object up the wound path until it emerged, all smeared with blood. A piece of bone.

Slocum let out a sigh and took a deep breath. He knew

now that the ball had splintered the large bone in the leg. He could do nothing about that. He tossed the splinter of bone aside and dug his finger back inside the wound. He found the same place where he had encountered the splinter and pushed downward until he felt the other hard object. He rubbed it with his finger and knew that he had found the bullet, lodged just beyond where it had smashed into the leg bone. He dug at it and pulled it toward him, rolling it ever so slowly along the path of the wound and where his knife had gone in a few moments before.

Travers squirmed but did not open his eyes. Slocum knew he must be experiencing a lot of pain even in his unconscious state. He kept fingering the chunk of lead, moving it ever closer to the entrance. Finally, it was close enough so that he put his thumb in and clamped the bullet between thumb and forefinger. He plucked the bloody slug out, examined it carefully. It was slightly misshapen from striking the bone, but only along one side. He looked to see if any of the lead had sheared off, but could not tell for sure. He hoped there wasn't a piece of lead still down in there, beyond his reach.

Travers was still out cold when Slocum cleaned his knife off by rubbing it up and down his trouser leg, sheathed it, then walked over to the fire and saw that the water was boiling. The bubbles bobbed and died and re-formed, sending up clouds of hot steam. Slocum found a pail used to hold oats and grain for the horses. He dipped it into the cauldron and rinsed it out, then filled it again.

He walked back over to Travers carrying the pail of scalding water. He drew a breath and braced himself. He knew the bottom of the pail would be hot to his touch for just a second or two while he upended it.

"This is going to hurt, Travers, but we've got to clean out that wound."

He knew Travers could not hear him, but he wanted him to know he was sorry for the pain he was going to cause him. Slocum quickly splashed the scalding water onto the wound with force enough to shoot a jet of water deep into the cavity where the bullet had been.

Travers came out of his swoon with a loud screech of pain. He grabbed his leg wound with both hands, then released them as the pain swept through him.

"It'll hurt for a minute, but I'm not through yet," Slocum said.

Travers cursed Slocum with a blue stream of invective that must have been lodged in his mind and throat for a long time just waiting to spew out.

"That'll clean out the wound, Travers," Slocum said. "Now, I've got to cauterize it."

"What? You sonofabitch, I can't stand the pain as it is."

"If I don't close that wound up, you'll leak all the way to Taos and won't have enough blood left in you to keep your heart going."

"What in hell's it mean, *cauterize*?"

"Burn that skin closed where the bullet went in."

"No," Travers said and tried to scoot away from Slocum.

Slocum said nothing, but drew his knife again and laid the blade on one of the stones so that it was directly in the fire. Then, he knelt down, hunched over, and blew on the fire to make it burn hotter against the blade.

Travers watched him with wide, fearful eyes. Slocum looked at him without expression on his face and saw that the young man was scared spitless.

"Take another pull on that whiskey if you want to, Travers. Or, I can knock you out again."

"I'm sick as it is from that stuff."

"It might help you stand the pain. It's going to be pretty fierce for a few minutes."

"You aren't touching me with that hot knife, Slocum."

Slocum smiled and pulled the knife from the flame. He walked over to Travers, who covered up his wound with both hands.

"I can burn right through them if you like, son," Slocum said.

Before Travers could answer, a voice spoke, seemingly out of nowhere.

"You get the hell away from him, mister, or I'll blow you plumb to hell."

Slocum froze as the hackles rose on the back of his neck, stiffened, and sent a cold chill down his spine.

Then, he heard the sound of a cocking hammer, and it was as loud as an iron door opening at the gates of hell.

# 4

Slocum turned slowly and saw the snout of a rifle poking out of the wagon. Behind it, at the other end of the barrel, he saw a face, just barely, peering at him from the shadows inside the covered wagon.

"Just back away, mister, or I'll put a bullet right through your black heart."

From the sound of the voice, Slocum couldn't tell if it was a man, boy, girl, or woman. The voice was pitched low, but did not have the gruffness he might associate with a male hard case.

Slocum backed away from Travers, without looking at him.

"Take it easy," Slocum said.

"Just drop that knife on the ground and walk away from it, towards me. Real easy, now."

"All right," Slocum said, dropping the knife at his feet. He turned slowly and took a step or two towards the wagon. He still could not clearly see the person who was hiding inside the wagon. But whoever it was had the drop on him, and he was in a dangerous position that could very well cost him his life if he made one false move.

"That's far enough, mister."

"I didn't mean any harm," Slocum said. "I was just trying to cauterize Ben's wound so he won't bleed to death."

"That's what you say. You might be in cahoots with those jaspers who jumped us."

"I'm not," Slocum said, looking over at Ben to see if the wounded man would back him up. Ben was passed out again. His eyes were closed and his head lolled on his left shoulder.

"Ben, do you trust this man?"

"He's knocked out," Slocum said.

"Is he alive?"

"Yes."

"I'm coming out. One false move from you, and I'll blow you to kingdom come."

"Come ahead," Slocum said.

He watched as the person climbed out of the wagon. He noticed that the muzzle of the rifle remained pointed at him the whole time. There was something about the person that didn't seem quite right, but he couldn't put a finger on it just yet. The person was slim and very agile. When the person stood on the ground and turned to face him, he was even more puzzled.

"Back away, mister. I want to see what you've done to my brother."

Slocum stepped to one side a couple of paces.

The person walked over to Ben and leaned down, put a finger to his neck, feeling for a pulse. A slender finger. Slocum looked closely at the hat on the person's head, then at the loose shirt. Then, it dawned on him.

"Why, you're nothing but a slip of a girl," he said.

"I ain't no girl, mister. I'm a woman, full growed, and I can shoot as well as any man."

"I don't doubt that. Now, are you going to let me cauterize Ben's wound or not? And that tourniquet's got to be loosened again or he'll lose his leg for sure."

The woman bent down and looked at the wound in Ben's leg. Slocum heard her gasp in alarm. She took her eyes off of him long enough for Slocum to lunge at her and grab the rifle from her hand. She rose up, flailing her fists at him, then trying to scratch his eyes out. Slocum stepped back, but she kept coming at him, attacking with her hands, kicking at his shins. He lifted one arm to ward off her blows, and she kicked him square in the groin.

Slocum doubled over in pain and he felt her hands knock his hat from his head, then grab his hair. She pulled hard and he felt strands of his hair strain at his scalp. He straightened up, and sidestepped her just as she kicked at his groin once again. Then, she loosened her grasp on his hair and started pounding his face with her fists. Slocum tried to back away, but she kept coming at him.

She reached for the rifle in Slocum's hand, and he swung his arm back away from her, throwing himself off balance. The woman twisted and drove her body into his, knocking Slocum down. She landed atop him, and they both struggled to gain the upper hand.

Slocum felt the pressure of her body atop his own, and he rolled over, pinning her beneath him. She squirmed to free herself, but he pinned one of her arms down and pressed against her so that she could not wriggle out from under him. He felt the heat of her loins against his own, and as he pinned her, he could feel her breasts pressing against his chest. He looked down into her eyes, saw the fierce light burning in them.

"You like this, don't you?" she asked.

"Not particularly."

"Then, let me up, you bastard."

"If you promise to behave."

"I wouldn't promise you the sweat off my brow," she said.

"Ma'am, I'm trying to save your brother's life, and there's not much time. If that tourniquet comes loose, he'll probably bleed to death, and if I don't loosen it some, that leg's going to mortify and I, or you, will have to cut it off."

"I don't believe you," she said.

"Damn you, lady. Your father's lying dead over yonder, and you should be grieving for him and leaving me to help your brother."

"That man isn't my father," she said.

"What?"

"He's my stepfather. Ben's my half brother. We have the same mother."

"Well, your stepfather needs washing up and burying. You could make yourself useful. Instead of being a pain in the ass."

"I don't trust you," she said, her mouth crumpling into a sullen pout.

"Too bad, lady. Because, right now, I'm the only one you can trust."

"I can't breathe, with you lying on top of me," she said.

"If you don't stop squirming, I might do more than that," Slocum said.

"What do you mean? Rape me?"

"I don't rape women. But the position I'm in would make it awful damned easy."

"You are a scoundrel, then. Like I thought."

Slocum smiled. Her eyes had softened somewhat, and he sensed she was no longer angry, or at least, not as angry as she had been when the fight started.

"It's women like you who make men into scoundrels."

Her mouth dropped open, and her eyes opened wide in a shocked stare.

"Well, aren't you the smug one, though? How dare you put the blame on women."

"You brought the subject up, lady."

"I did no such thing."

"Well, we're not going anywhere, and Ben might die or lose his leg while you argue with me."

"Let me up."

"And, if I do, you'll stay out of my hair?"

"I'd like to tear your hair out by the roots," she said.

"That's not a good answer, Missy."

"I'd like to be able to breathe again."

"You can breathe all right if I knock you out, you know."

"You've already proven you'd hit a woman."

"I haven't hit you yet," Slocum said.

"Well, you've pushed me around."

"If I hit you, you'll know it," he said.

She squirmed beneath him again, and Slocum pressed harder to keep her pinned. His prick had begun to harden, however, and he was sure she could feel it nudging against her most private place. In fact, she sighed, and lifted her hips to keep the pressure up. Either, he thought, she was begging him to take her, or she was teasing him just to see what he was made of.

"The longer you keep me busy with you," Slocum said, "the shorter your brother's life gets. You might want to think about that."

"Let me up," she said. "I promise I won't cause any more trouble. Unless you do something to Ben that kills him."

"Fair enough. But, before I let you up, what's your name?"

"Are you trying to start a romance?" she taunted.

"I just want to know what to call you in case I need you to help me with Ben."

"My name is Eleanor. They call me Ellie. And, what's your name, big boy?"

There was a smirk on her lips when she asked this, and Slocum almost didn't answer.

"Slocum," he said. "John Slocum."

"Is that your real name? Or one you made up so you could rob people?"

"That's the name I was born with down in Calhoun County, Georgia."

"So, you're a damned rebel."

"Nope, Ellie. I'm just another American. Like you."

"Let me up," she said.

Slocum released his grip on Ellie's arm and rolled away from her. But he was careful to get up first, and he still held on to her rifle.

"Do you need any help with Ben?" she asked, dusting herself off.

"No. Just stay out of my hair. Tend to your stepfather, unless you're squeamish about such things."

She looked down at his crotch.

"I guess you have a short memory," she mocked. "Is that all you're short of?"

"Maybe. Now go."

She walked toward the dead man, and Slocum went over to Ben and picked up his knife. He put the blade into the fire once again and waited while he watched Ellie turn over the body of her stepfather.

When the knife blade was heated through, leaving a blue streak on the silvery iron shaft, Slocum quickly placed it over Ben's open wound. At the same time, he loosened the tourniquet on the young man's leg.

There was the smell and sizzle of flesh as the hot blade sealed over the wound. Ben jerked up out of unconsciousness long enough to scream out in pain. Slocum pushed him back down with his left hand.

"Easy now," Slocum said. "You don't want to open that wound back up."

"I-I can't stand the pain," Ben gasped.

"You can stand a lot more than that. And this pain won't last long. Just ride it out, son."

Ellie rushed over and stood looking down at the two men.

"Ben," she said, "can I help?"

"No-no, I-I'll be all right. But, boy, it hurts like hell."

"I see you cauterized his wound," Ellie said.

"Look at that leg where the tourniquet was. I don't like the looks of it."

"What do you mean?" Ben asked.

"I just hope the blood starts flowing again. It will help with the healing."

"You'd better hope it does, Slocum," Ellie said. "If anything happens to Ben. . . ."

"Don't go jumping to conclusions," Slocum said. "I warned you about that tourniquet being tight for so long."

"Just the same," Ellie said, "what you did to Ben had damned sure better work."

"Ellie, please," Ben said, "I-I'll be all right in a few minutes. I'm sure Slocum did what he thought was best."

"Maybe you'd better tend to your stepfather," Slocum told Ellie. "We'll have to bury him here."

"I'm going to take him back to Taos," Ben said.

"He won't last that long, Ben," Slocum said. "Best to bury him here, mark the spot. You can always come back with a casket and bring him home."

"I think he's right," Ellie said.

Slocum looked at her, surprised that she had come to his defense. She scowled at him and walked away, heading toward the body of her stepfather.

"Slocum," Ben said. "Come close. There's something I've got to tell you."

Slocum scooted closer to the wounded man, noting the tightness in his speech. He could tell that Ben was in a great deal of pain.

"What is it?" Slocum asked.

"If-if something happens to me—I mean, if I don't make it . . ."

"You'll make it, Ben. I got the bullet out. That raises your chances."

"But, if I don't make it back to Taos, there are some things you ought to know. Something I'd like you to do for me."

Ben spoke in a whisper so that Ellie would not hear him, and Slocum noted that, too. He leaned closer to Ben so that he could hear what he had to say.

"I don't know if I can trust you or not, but I feel like I can."

"That's something you've got to work out for yourself."

"I've got to get a message to my sister."

"Ellie?"

"No, my real sister, Bettilee Travers. Ellie is my half sister."

"Don't you trust Ellie?" Slocum asked.

Ben shook his head, then grimaced in pain from the movement.

"No, but I can't tell you why just yet. There's something funny about us getting jumped like that, and my father getting killed."

Slocum sensed the bitterness in Ben's voice. He wondered what there was between Ben and Ellie that he had to keep secrets from her. And what did he suspect about the bushwhackers?

"Go on," Slocum said.

"Bettilee is unmarried and now all alone. Please, Slocum, help her, will you?"

"What's the message, Ben?"

Just as Ben opened his mouth to tell Slocum what was on his mind, they both were startled to hear Ellie cry out.

"He's not dead," Ellie screamed. "Slocum, get the hell over here."

"Go on," Ben said. "My father needs you if he's still alive."

"I'll do what I can," Slocum said, as he rose to his feet.

But he didn't put much faith in Ellie's observation. Sometimes a dead person expelled a last breath when they were moved and could give the impression of still being alive.

But there was a small chance that Ellie was right.

And he hoped she was, so that he wouldn't have to keep another man's secret.

# 5

Slocum knelt down beside Ellie and bent over the elder Travers. He put his ear close to the man's slightly open mouth, listening for any faint sound of breathing. He put two fingers on the man's neck, right on the carotid artery, feeling for any pulse.

"Where did you learn to do all this?" Ellie asked, slightly breathless.

"Shh," Slocum said.

It was true, Ben's father was still alive, but just barely. Slocum detected a very slight pulse, and he could hear air going in and out of the man's mouth, but his breathing was so shallow, Slocum wondered if he could ever recover.

He sat up and examined the elder Travers. There were two bullet holes that he could see, one right next to the heart, the other on the other side of the chest. It was his guess that the man had been shot in both lungs and was just barely hanging on to life.

"Well?" Ellie asked.

"He is alive, if you want to call it that. I don't know how. He's got a bullet near his heart that almost certainly tore up his left lung and another in the center of the right lung. He's a goner, for sure."

"Is there nothing you can do for him?" she asked.

"No," Slocum said. "When you turned him over, it might have made it easier for him to breathe. But just a little. He's just about to go. Any minute now."

"How do you know? Are you some kind of doctor?"

"I'm not," Slocum said.

"But you know something about medicine."

"I know something about death."

"You were in the war," she said flatly.

"Yes."

"No need to ask which side you were on, I guess."

"It's not important. It was a bad war, and I saw a lot of men die. It looks to me like someone deliberately shot your stepfather."

"What do you mean?"

"I mean, whoever shot him, shot to kill. Deliberately. Those bullet holes are too close together. They're right on a line with each other. One was meant for the heart, the other was meant to stop him from ever breathing again."

"You make it sound so-so cold and calculating."

"I'd say it was done in cold blood," Slocum said.

"These were not wild shots fired in the heat of battle. My guess is that your stepfather here was shot first by somebody who wanted him dead right off."

"Yes. I heard him cry out. He was hit first, and he went down right away. I was inside the wagon, and I lay down flat so I wouldn't get shot. It took me awhile to find my rifle, and by that time, you had chased those bushwhackers off."

Just then, the wounded man gasped and both Ellie and Slocum heard him expel air from his lungs. Then, his chest seemed to cave in and the bleeding from his wounds stopped.

"Is he . . . ?" Ellie struggled to ask the question.

"Yes," Slocum said. "He's dead."

"Are you sure?" she asked.

"I'm sure. You may want to clean him up, put another shirt on him. I'll dig him a grave when I finish with Ben."

"Yes," Ellie said, a far-off look in her eyes, "I-I want to clean him up, give him a proper burial. You take care of Benny."

Slocum went back to Ben, who was still gritting his teeth in pain.

"Is my father dead?" Ben asked.

"He could not have lived, even if he had been shot in a surgeon's office. I'm sorry."

"For a minute there, I thought there might be some hope."

Tears welled up in Ben's eyes and then streamed down his cheek. But he drew in a deep breath and fought off his grief.

"Listen, Slocum. I've got to get this off my chest. It's important."

"You go right ahead," Slocum said. "Ellie will be busy for a while, and then I've got to bury your father."

"I wish I could help."

"You just take it easy," Slocum said.

"Come close, Slocum. I don't want Ellie to hear what I've got to say."

Slocum squatted down next to Ben and leaned close.

"I have a map," Ben whispered. "It's in a strongbox in the wagon. When you get to Taos, if I'm not alive, give that map to Bettilee."

"A map?" Slocum asked.

"It's in a locked strongbox in the wagon. The key is in my pocket. If I die, dig that key out and get the map. Give the map to Bettilee."

"You'll give it to her yourself, I'm sure. Don't give up just yet."

"I feel funny about this, Slocum. Maybe I was meant to die with my father."

Slocum said nothing. Ben was feeling badly, and he'd seen that in men before, too. Sometimes it made all the difference toward recovery—how a man felt. He'd seen men die of slight wounds, while others, more seriously wounded, fought back and lived to fight another day.

"The map will lead Bettilee to our father's mine near Taos. He's been mining there for three years and the ore kept getting richer. When he took some ore to get assayed in Santa Fe, they asked a lot of questions and Pa got suspicious. They asked him where his mine was, and so we brought some more ore up to Pueblo to have it assayed there."

"And?" Slocum asked.

"The ore was very rich. So the mine is worth a fortune."

"Why don't you trust Ellie? You and your father brought her along on this trip."

"Pa brought her along because he doesn't trust her. And she and Bettilee don't get along. Pa thinks Ellie wants the mine for herself. But she doesn't know where it is, and she doesn't know what the assay report said."

"So she doesn't know that the ore was rich," Slocum said.

"No. It was richer than we expected. Pa and I have quite a bit of ore already mined and hidden away. Now we can take it to the smelter and become wealthy. Or, at least, that's what Pa planned before he was killed."

The mention of his father's death brought more tears to Ben's eyes. But Slocum could see that there was more he wanted to say.

"So, what is Bettilee going to say when you tell her about the mine, and all the ore you've hidden away?"

"She'll be surprised if I tell her. If you tell her, she won't believe you. She never believed in our pa's mine."

"Why won't she believe me if I give her the map?"

"She'll think you killed me and my pa. She's even more of a suspicious sort than our pa was."

"So you have to give her the map yourself."

"But, if I don't make it back to Taos, you have to promise me you'll give her the map. It has things on there that only she knows. The map would do you no good, nor Ellie. Pa made it so that only Bettilee has the key to where the mine and the silver are."

"But, if she doesn't trust me. . . ."

"Slocum, there's a locket around my neck. With her picture in it. If you take that to her and tell her I gave it to you, she'll believe you came to help."

"Why would she do that?" Slocum asked.

Ben looked around furtively before he spoke again. Then he pulled Slocum close so that he could whisper even more softly.

"Because," Ben said, "because I'm going to tell you about the locket."

Ben reached up and opened his shirt. He plucked the locket from its resting place on his chest and held it in his hand. He pressed a small flange on the side and the face of the locket popped open to reveal the face of a beautiful young woman.

"That's Bettilee?" Slocum asked.

Ben nodded. "This locket is made from the first ore me and my pa took from the mine. It's nigh a hunnert percent pure silver."

Ben closed the locket and slipped it back under his shirt. "If I don't make it, Slocum, you show Bettilee this locket and give her the map."

"You'll give that map to her yourself, I expect," Slocum said.

"But you promise you'll do it if I don't make it back."

"I promise," Slocum said. Then, he stood up. "I'm going to help Ellie bury your father, then we've got to load you in the wagon and make some miles while we still have light."

"I'm ready to leave whenever you are," Ben said.

Slocum helped Ellie put a clean shirt on her stepfather. It was a grisly task, but she didn't cringe from it.

"Poor Ethan," she said, when she finished buttoning the clean shirt.

"Were you and he close?" Slocum asked.

"Not very. I think he carried a grudge against my father for having been married to my mother."

"What happened to her?" Slocum asked.

"Her name was Daphne," Ellie said. "She ran off about three years ago."

"Ran off?"

"Disappeared. Ethan, Bettilee, Ben, and I went into town one day and when we came back she was gone. Broke poor Ethan's heart. And us kids cried our eyes out for two weeks."

"And you don't know what happened to her, or why she left?"

"Ethan blames my father. Blamed, I mean. He thinks my pa came back and took her away."

"What do you think?"

"I think our mother still carried a torch for my father."

"What was his name?"

"Jesse. Jesse Dunbar."

"And you haven't seen him since he left your mother?"

"No."

Slocum said nothing, but he thought it was mighty strange that her father left a wife and child and never bothered to look in on either one of them.

Ellie brought Slocum a well-worn shovel and, together, they found a suitable place to bury Ethan Travers. Slocum dug a shallow grave, shallow because he struck hard rock about a foot or so down and couldn't get around it. He and Ellie placed Travers body face up in the grave. She folded his arms across his chest and then covered him with an old moth-eaten blanket she dug out of the wagon. She walked over to talk to Ben while Slocum shoveled dirt over the corpse. When he had finished, he placed rocks over the mound of dirt to keep the animals away, he hoped, until the family could return and carry Travers back to Taos for a proper burial.

He leaned the shovel against one of the wagon wheels and walked over to speak to Ben and Ellie.

"Better load you in the wagon, Ben," Slocum said. "I'll tie my horse to it and drive you and Ellie back to Taos. You feel up to being moved?"

"I reckon. My leg hurts like fire."

"I'll take another look at it tonight, put a bandage on it. You just lie still and yell out if that wound breaks open.

Ellie, make him as soft a bed as you can, so he doesn't bounce around too much."

"I already have a soft bed in the wagon for you, Ben."

Ellie and Slocum carried Ben over to the wagon. She pulled down the tailgate, and they helped Ben up into the wagon bed. Slocum climbed up and pulled the young man inside. Ellie came inside and made Ben comfortable.

Slocum unsaddled his horse, put the saddle, saddlebags, bridle, and bedroll inside the wagon. He slipped a halter over the gelding and roped him to one of the wagon struts. He carried his rifle up front and climbed into the seat, picked up the reins, slipped off the break. He looked back inside the covered wagon to see if Ellie and Ben were ready.

"Here we go," he said.

"Thank you, Slocum," Ben said. "Thank you for burying my pa."

Slocum nodded, but said nothing. He was hoping he wouldn't have to bury Ben somewhere on the long trail to Taos. And he didn't much like Ellie being behind him, with that rifle of hers. He thought he could trust her about as far as he could throw that noisy, rumbling, clanking excuse for a wagon that he found himself hitched to like the borrowed horse following them at the end of a rope.

# 6

Slocum drove the wagon at a steady pace, keeping his
eyes on the road ahead and looking for places where they
might be ambushed. But the land was desolate and almost
monotonous. He was glad, therefore, when, after two
hours of straining his eyes and wondering if a bushwhacker's bullet might whine out of nowhere and find
him, Ellie slipped out of the back of the wagon and onto
the seat beside him.

"Ben's asleep," she said.

"That's good, maybe."

"He-he's awful hot. I mean he's really sweating."

"Fever?"

"Yes. He's running a fever."

"That could be either good or bad," Slocum said.

"What do you mean?"

"The fever could be burning out the poison that's in
him from that bullet wound. Or it could mean something
else."

"Something else?"

"An infection in his leg. I've seen men get high fevers and pull through. And, I've also seen men . . ."

"In the war, you mean."

"Yes."

"How can we tell the difference with Ben?"

"We'll just have to wait and see," Slocum said.

Ellie sighed and shaded her eyes as she looked around at the landscape passing by. "It's awful hot back in the wagon. Maybe that's why Ben is feverish."

"Maybe."

"You don't know any more than I do about this, do you, Slocum?"

"No. I'm not a doctor."

"What are you?"

"Just a man, Ellie."

"I know that. I could tell when you were lying on top of me back there. What else? Are you an outlaw?"

"That's a hard question to answer," he said.

"Why? Are you wanted by the law?"

"Back home in Calhoun County, Georgia, I probably am."

"Why?"

"It's a long story," Slocum said. "And it happened a long time ago. After the war."

"I thought there was something about you that was, well, dangerous. Suspicious."

"You think too much, Ellie."

"I'm curious about you, Slocum. There are just too many things about you that don't add up."

"Maybe you should give up using arithmetic on me."

Ellie laughed.

"You have a way with words, too."

"I'm not a criminal, if that relieves your mind a little. I don't ride the outlaw trail."

"I'm not so sure about that," she said.

"Let's just change the subject, shall we, Ellie? I'm trying to be a Good Samaritan, and maybe we should just leave it at that."

"What did you and Ben talk about back there? The silver mine?"

"You ask too many questions, young lady. Whatever Ben and I talked about is our business, not yours."

She was silent then and, for a while, all they heard was the creak of the wagon and the sound of Ben's labored breathing. Slocum knew that Ben was probably fighting off infection, struggling against the effects of the wound in his leg. The next few hours, he knew, would tell the tale. If Ben fought off the infection, he had a good chance of surviving the bullet wound. If not, gangrene could set in, and he would die a horrible, agonizing death.

As for Ellie's questions about his being an outlaw, Slocum had wry thoughts about that issue. When he returned to his home in the Allegheny mountains in Calhoun County, Georgia, after the war in 1866, it was to find his mother and father both dead. His wound-weakened father had succumbed to a wasting disease and his grief-stricken mother had followed him soon after. Not only that, but he discovered that his family's farm had been seized by carpetbaggers working under the umbrella of Reconstruction Georgia, and that, he thought, had been the final insult not only to the South, but to him, and all Confederate soldiers who had fought bravely and honorably in a vile war.

He had killed his first man while no longer wearing a uniform, a gunman hired to enforce the seizure of the

Slocum farm, a man bent on killing him. And he had also shot and killed the crooked county judge who rode out to serve papers on him. Slocum had ridden away from home, headed West, knowing he was a man wanted for murder, that he had been sentenced to death in absentia. So, in that sense, he supposed, he was an outlaw, but he had not ridden the owlhoot trail and his conscience was clear.

Reconstruction was a diabolical nightmare, a bad law that allowed unscrupulous persons to seize land and property belonging to decent, law-abiding citizens. He had been bitter, but until Ellie had brought it up, he had come to terms with his past and had learned to live with that shadow of a death sentence dogging him all over the West.

He supposed he could be considered an outlaw by some. But the war was long over and it was time that old grudges be buried and forgotten. Certainly he had tried to do that, even though he still rankled at the injustice of Reconstruction.

As the afternoon shadows grew long, Slocum began scouting for a place where they might camp for the night. Ellie had gone back inside the wagon several times to tend to her brother, whose fever was raging. She watered cloths and placed them on his sweaty forehead to try and bring his temperature down.

Finally, Slocum spotted an ideal place to set up camp for the night. He drove the wagon off the main trail and into a grove of stunted junipers and pines, a place that afforded both shelter and concealment and could be defended easily.

"Is this where we're stopping for the night?" Ellie asked, as Slocum drove the wagon into the trees.

"Yes. It would be dangerous to travel this road at night."

"Good. I'm weary to the bone and Ben's not doing too good."

"Some whiskey might help break his fever. I'll look at him later. First, let's erase our wagon tracks in here, just in case somebody's trying to track us."

"How?"

"I'll cut some pine branches and we can use them like a broom, sweep away the marks of the wagon wheels."

"Sounds like a good idea," Ellie said.

"It won't fool a good tracker, but in the dark, it might give us a few minutes warning in case somebody comes prowling around."

Slocum cut two juniper boughs and gave one to Ellie. Together, they swept away all traces of the wagon leaving the main road. Slocum walked back and made sure the sweeping did not show, adding bits of brush and wood to the earth where it had been cleaned.

"How's Ben doing?" he asked when he returned to the wagon hidden in the trees.

"You'd better take a look at him," Ellie said. "He's very pale and his lips are cracked from the fever. I tried to get him to drink some water, but he only moaned and pushed my hand away."

"We'll have to get him to drink," Slocum said, as he climbed up into the wagon.

He felt Ben's forehead and neck. They were both hot to the touch. Then he looked at the wound in Ben's leg to see if it was festering. The cauterized flesh was holding, but it was red and hot around the wound. Not a good sign, Slocum thought. He picked up the canteen Ellie had used and held Ben up, poured a little water on his lips. He pried open Ben's mouth and poured some water on his tongue, careful not to pour so much that he choked him.

"Feel bad," Ben said.

"You'll have to ride it out, son," Slocum said. "Maybe the fever will break tonight."

Ben closed his eyes and said no more.

Slocum told Ellie that he thought it best they not make a fire, just have a dry camp. She nodded in agreement.

"I'll lay out my bedroll over yonder," Slocum said, "so I can keep an eye on the wagon and the road. You'll sleep inside with Ben."

"Yes," Ellie said. "We have some jerky and cold beans, some hardtack. Will that be enough for you?"

"Yes," Slocum said, grabbing his bedroll and climbing out of the wagon.

While Ellie gathered together the grub, Slocum set up his bedroll behind a small rise about fifty feet from the wagon. There he had a good view of the road and the wagon, while his site was concealed from view.

Slocum and Ellie ate silently. She had some canned peaches which she opened, and it made a fine topping to the dry meal. "What about Ben?" she asked. "Should I try to get him to eat something?"

"No, not unless he asks for food. Sleep is the best thing for him right now. And, for you, too, Ellie."

She shot him a grateful look. "You can be nice when you want to be," she said.

Slocum said nothing. He knew she had been studying him while they ate and he had to admit, he had been studying her, too. Her manly clothes could not quite conceal that she was a good looking woman. He knew she would look pretty in a dress. She had sharp features, a fine straight nose, good white teeth, and a becoming smile.

But she had a lot of anger in her and probably had a lot of doubts about him, just as he had about her.

"Keep your rifle handy tonight," Slocum said. "I'm going to turn in. But I sleep light, so I'll surely hear if anyone tries to sneak up on us in the darkness."

"I'm a light sleeper, too," she said, and there seemed to be some undercurrent of coyness in her tone.

"Good night," Slocum said and carried his rifle over to his bedroll. He wore a big Colt on his hip and had his hideout gun, as well as a knife. He took his saddlebags with him, too, so that he had plenty of ammunition handy.

He heard Ellie climb into the wagon as he lay down. It wasn't long before the sun fell behind the mountains and plunged the road and trees into darkness.

Bullbats knifed the air chasing after flying insects and, in the distance, a lone coyote yipped and then broke into full chromatic cry as Slocum drifted into a shallow sleep, his ears still registering the sounds of night. The tiredness seeped through his muscles and bones and his eyelids grew heavy despite his best intentions.

Sometime later, when the moon was high in the velvet night sky, Slocum felt a hot breath at his cheek. His eyes popped wide open, but he saw only a shadow in front of his face.

Then he felt a soft cold hand on his belly and the hand moved against the buckle of his belt and he heard the slither of leather, the snap of metal as the buckle came undone. Then, quick, eager fingers slid the buttons of his fly through the eyelets and the hand slid down into his crotch, and he felt fingers close around his cock, draw it out, stroke it smoothly.

"Slocum," Ellie whispered into his ear, "I kept thinking

about this, and I couldn't sleep. I wanted to see for myself
if it was as big as it felt."

"Ellie, you're a caution. Is it?"

"I don't know yet. I want you inside me. Now."

He reached out for her, her silhouette outlined against
the pale brightness of the moon and he knew she wore
only a light housecoat and it was open and she was naked.
He felt her breasts as she leaned down to kiss him and
the nipples grew hard under the caress of his fingertips.

"John Slocum," she husked, "how quick can you get
your clothes off? I want you real bad."

"Quick as you get off me, Ellie."

"No sooner said than done," she said, sliding off him.
She turned around and started pulling off his boots while
Slocum shed his shirt. She tugged his trousers down and
tossed them in a heap, and then he was on her and she
took him inside her with a willingness that did not surprise
him.

He pumped her and she thrashed with pleasure, urging
him on with hot whispers in his ear, begging him to give
it all to her. Slocum obliged with relish and pounded into
her with a force that pinned her beneath him and elicited
cries of delight.

"Oh yes," she cooed, "you're big, John Slocum and I
love it, love it."

She bowed her back, and then elevated her hips and he
drove in even deeper than before. She clawed his back
like a wildcat, and the stars spun silently above them on
a slow carousel against an inky sky.

"Now," she screamed into his ear and Slocum drove
on, taking her higher and higher until he exploded his
balls inside her, and she bucked beneath him, her body
slick with the sweat of their lovemaking.

He kissed her then, hard on her lips, and she let out a long grateful sigh and reached down for him, kneading the softening flesh of his manhood until it stood rigid.

"I want you again," she whispered. "I can't get enough of you, John Slocum."

"Maybe, like me," he said, "it's been too long."

"Yes, yes . . . way too long."

And Slocum took her again in the great deep silence of the night.

# 7

Slocum awoke before dawn, startled and surprised that he had fallen so deeply asleep. He was stark naked and shivering in the cold that came to the plains and foothills even in the middle of summer.

Ellie was gone and he was not surprised, for he had told her she must return to the wagon and tend to her brother. But he had no idea when she had left. She had said good night to him and turned him over, and he had fallen asleep almost immediately, the musk of her still in his nostrils, the heat of her still on his naked body.

His clothing was cold, and he shivered as he dressed in the predawn darkness. He had to guard against his teeth chattering, but as it was, he could not hear much because he was breathing heavily with the exertion of pulling on his boots and strapping on his pistol. He warmed his small hideout pistol before tucking it next to the inside of his belt, right up against his bare skin.

Slocum packed up his bedroll and walked back to the wagon by a different route from the way he had come.

He entered the clump of trees and stopped to listen. The silence was deep, and he heard nothing unusual. He walked closer to the wagon and stopped once again. He listened intently and could hear the sound of someone breathing heavily. He listened long enough to know that he could hear two people breathing.

Satisfied, Slocum approached the wagon and set his bedroll by one of the rear wagon wheels. He fished out a small cigar, lit it, and walked away with his rifle in hand to wait for the sun to rise. There was no use waking Ellie at that hour. They would have a long drive today.

Slocum finished smoking his small cheroot and wished he had a cup of coffee to start the day. The sky in the east began to pale and Slocum heard sounds from the wagon. Movement, as if someone was awake and getting dressed.

Moments later, the sounds stopped and then he saw Ellie climbing out of the back of the wagon. She was wearing her traveling clothes, a pair of pants, boots, a shirt, and a man's hat. He waited until she was standing next to the wagon and then cleared his throat.

"Slocum? That you?"

"Yes," he said, his voice just barely above a whisper.

She walked over to him. "I missed you in my bed," she said, sidling up to him.

"It was cold waking up without you, Ellie."

She laughed.

"Walk out to the road with me, will you?" Slocum asked.

"What's up?"

"I don't know. A feeling. I just want to see if we had anyone prowling around during the night. I kind of failed in my duties."

"Your duties?"

"To watch over you and Ben. I fell sound asleep."

"You earned that sleep, John," she said, linking her arm in his. "You're some man."

As the sky lightened, Slocum could see the ground where he and Ellie had smoothed it out with pine branches. Only, it was no longer trackless. There was the track of a coyote, and more ominous, a man's boot. Slocum knelt down to study it.

The man had left a deep boot print, so he was probably packing some weight. The track was fresh, less than an hour old. The sole of the boot had some nicks in it, as if the man had walked on sharp stones, cutting the leather.

Slocum stood up. "Go back to the wagon, Ellie, and wait. I'm going to look around and see if I can't find where that bunch waited while this jasper came by this morning looking for us."

"I want to stay with you," she said.

"Why?"

"Maybe the tracks will tell me something, too."

"You're a tracker?" Slocum asked.

"No. Not like you. But one of those horses looked familiar to me."

"What do you mean?"

"I think I may have seen one of the horses before," she said.

"Where? In Pueblo? In Taos?"

Ellie shook her head. "I don't know. Somewhere. That buckskin. Did you see it?"

"Yes. There was a buckskin, a dappled gray, and a sorrel. I saw the horses right well."

"Just let me go with you, John."

"All right. But be quiet and if you hear any noise or a shot, you hit the ground. Hear?"

"Yes."

Slocum started backtracking the boot prints. They led down the road a short distance in the way they had come to their night stop, and then they left the road. The land pitched off at that point and was below the roadway, so anyone could have ridden by without being seen from the copse of trees.

Whoever had been there, was no longer there. Slocum studied the land in all directions and saw nothing out of the ordinary, nothing moving.

He found the place where the two other men had waited. There were hoofprints all around a small area. He found a crushed cigarette butt, then another. He found a place where one of the men had lit down and urinated. He studied the three different sets of tracks very carefully. There was no way of telling which track belonged to which horse, but one of the sets of tracks bore a distinctive mark on the right rear hoof. The shoe had a slight nick in it.

"Have you ever seen that track before, Ellie?" Slocum asked, pointing to the nicked shoe print.

"No," she said, after looking hard at the track.

"But you don't usually look at horseshoe tracks, do you?" he asked.

Ellie shook her head.

"No matter. Until he puts new shoes on, we'll know the track next time we see it."

"Do you think we'll see those men again, John?"

"I would bet money on it," Slocum said.

Back at the wagon, Ellie climbed in to look at Ben

while Slocum grained the horses, made preparations to get back on the road.

"How's your brother?" he asked when Ellie emerged from the covered wagon. "Did his fever break during the night?"

"No, I'm afraid not. John, I'm worried. He's awake, but he's not himself."

"I'll take a look."

Slocum climbed up into the wagon. Ellie came in, too, knelt beside Slocum. He felt Ben's clothes. They were damp with sweat. He looked at the wound he had cauterized and saw that it had broken up slightly, just enough for blood and fluid to seep through.

"This is not good," he said to Ellie. "He's been rubbing at his wound."

"I didn't know," she said.

"We'll wrap it and hope it heals over again. But it might get infected, nevertheless. Do you have any medicines here?"

"No. Not even horse salve."

"Damn. Well, keep an eye on him. Give him plenty of water. We'll stop every so often so I can take a look at that leg."

"I can look at it, if you tell me what to do."

"Look for any blue streaks going up his leg. See if the smell of it changes any."

"I'll do that," she said.

"Then, let's go. I'll hook up the horses. You stay here with Ben, and we'll move out."

Slocum worked fast and in less than a half an hour he was turning the team back onto the road heading south for Taos. The wagon rumbled over the rough road, and Slocum's stomach growled with hunger. But he was intent on watching the way ahead and places where they might expect an ambush. Somehow, he had the feeling that they were being watched, but that they weren't going to be attacked out there in the open and so soon after they had gotten back under way.

He pondered over Ellie's telling him about the buckskin horse. That was mighty odd, and she hadn't volunteered any further information. Perhaps she didn't know where she had seen the horse before, but it was Slocum's strong hunch that she did know more about it than she was telling.

He had the feeling that Ellie was now filled with regret that she had even mentioned having seen the buckskin horse before. Perhaps, he thought, she had remembered where she had seen the horse and now was sorry she had brought it up. If so, she was hiding something, and he didn't like that a damned bit.

"Water, water," Ben cried out, and Slocum turned in his seat to look back into the wagon.

"Ellie . . ." Slocum said.

"He's delirious, John," Ellie said. "I've been trying to force water into his mouth, but he fights me off."

"Ben, can you hear me?" Slocum asked.

"Pa, give me some water," Ben raved, and Slocum's brow furrowed with worry. This was not a good sign. Ben's fever should have broken during the night, and he should be well enough to eat and drink. Instead, he seemed to have worsened. Slocum now wondered if he had gotten all of the pieces of lead out of Ben's leg.

"We'll stop up here, and I'll take a look at him," Slocum said. "Try and keep him quiet and keep pushing water out of that canteen."

"I'll try," Ellie said.

Slocum found a wide spot and pulled the wagon over, set the brake. Before he climbed into the back of the wagon, he looked all around just to make sure they weren't being watched. But the land was broken with rocky spires and small buttes, hillocks, vegetation. There was no safe place, he realized. Those bushwhackers could be anywhere. To his right, the foothills of the Rocky Mountains rose up in ever higher levels, and a man could set up there and see one hell of a long way.

For the moment, though, Slocum saw no cause for alarm, and he would take a chance that they were safe for the time being. He turned and crawled into the wagon, came up beside Ben.

"He looks terrible, doesn't he, John?" Ellie said.

"Damn," Slocum said. "That wound has broken open again, and he's leaking pus and blood."

"I-I hadn't noticed," Ellie said. "Is that bad?"

"It means he's got an infection inside his leg. Where's that bottle of whiskey?"

"I put it back in your saddlebag. I gave Ben a little of it last night to help him sleep."

"Dig it out."

Ellie handed Slocum the bottle of whiskey that was still more than half full. His mouth watered, but he knew this wasn't the time for him to take a taste. He popped the cork and poured a small amount of the whiskey into Ben's open and suppurating wound. Ben half rose up and screamed in pain. Slocum pushed him back down.

"What did you do that for?" Ellie asked.

"The alcohol in whiskey is a disinfectant. Maybe it will knock out the infection in Ben's leg."

"I hate to see him like that—in such pain."

"If that infection takes hold, he'll have worse pain than this, Ellie."

Ben struggled with Slocum, but was soon exhausted and lay still, his eyes still wide with pain and fear.

"Pour some of this whiskey in about every hour, Ellie. If you need help, give me a holler, and I'll come back and hold Ben down."

"All right," Ellie said, pouting.

"Now, we'd best get moving again. I don't like this place much. We're right at the upward slope of a grade, which makes us ripe for another ambush."

Slocum crawled back outside onto the seat and was about to release the brake and get started again when he heard the crack of a rifle and the high-pitched whine of a bullet searing the air over his head. Slocum ducked and reached for his Winchester rifle. Two more shots rang out and he heard both bullets thud into the side of the wagon, splintering wood.

Slocum jacked a cartridge into the chamber of the lever action rifle and peered over the top of seat, looking for a target.

"They're all around us," Ellie shouted from inside the wagon. "I'm coming out."

"No, stay where you are," Slocum said as he saw a rider appear on the slope to his right. Slocum swung his rifle to bear on the shooter, but just as he fired, the rider disappeared behind a high cairn of rocks. His bullet spanged off the rocks, showered sparks and fragments into the air.

Then he saw another man toward his left and levered another cartridge into the chamber.

As he fired, Slocum wondered silently. "Where in hell is that other bushwhacker?"

Another shot cracked from a rifle, and Slocum had his answer.

# 8

Slocum fired too quickly as he ducked. Wood splintered near his head, and he knew he was flanked on both sides by at least three men firing at him and the wagon.

Ellie crawled out of the wagon and peered over the top of the wagon skirts. She had her rifle with her and fired it as Slocum reloaded the chamber of his Winchester and scooted around to see if he had a shot at the last man to fire at him.

"There's that buckskin horse again," Slocum said, taking aim on the rider.

"I see him," Ellie said. Slocum fired as the man on the galloping buckskin, knowing he had not led his horse hard enough, gained speed. A moment later, Slocum heard her exclaim: "Oh my God!"

"What's the matter?" Slocum asked.

Before she could answer, another rifle barked and a bullet tore through the top of the canvas, just above both their heads.

"I'm going to climb out," Slocum said, "and see if I can't find better cover."

"I'll cover you," she said, firing off another round.

Slocum fired another round off at the nearest attacker and scrambled out of the wagon, sprawling facedown beside the left front wheel. He crabbed around the wheel and crawled underneath and rose to his feet on the other side, a fresh shell in the chamber. He saw the rider twist and turn his way. Slocum drew a tight bead on the man and, as he turned to face Slocum, Slocum squeezed the trigger. He saw the man jerk as the bullet slammed him in his chest, square in the middle of his breastbone. Blood sprayed out as the man's arms went high in the air, and his rifle went flying.

That was the man, Slocum noted, on the dappled gray. The man tried to hold on to the saddle horn as his horse twisted in confusion, but his grip on life was too short, and he toppled from the saddle and fell to the ground with a loud thud. Slocum walked up to the head of the team of horses and saw another flanker yelling to the man on the buckskin.

"He got Chris," the man yelled. "He's plumb dead."

"Let's light a shuck," said the man on the buckskin.

"You'll pay for that, mister," the man shouted at Slocum. "You'll pay in kind, you bastard."

With that, the man on the sorrel turned his horse and galloped over the high point of the road. The man on the buckskin took a last look at Slocum and rode off in the same direction, leaving a curtain of dust in his wake.

Slocum walked over to the man he had shot. He heard a noise behind him and turned to see Ellie climbing down out of the wagon, her rifle in her left hand. He didn't wait for her, but continued on toward the fallen man.

Slocum turned and saw that Ellie was running toward him at high speed. He wondered why. He did not have long to dwell on that thought however, as he stepped up to the man on the ground. The man they had called Chris was staring up at Slocum with sightless eyes. The hole in his chest was no longer pumping blood, but he had lost a great deal before he took his final breath.

"John," Ellie gasped, as she ran up to him. "Is he dead?"

"Yes."

Ellie looked down at the dead man.

"Oh my God," she breathed and then sank to her knees as if they had suddenly turned to jelly.

"You know this man?" Slocum asked.

For a moment, Slocum thought Ellie had been struck dumb. Her mouth opened, but no sound came out. Then she sucked in a breath, and it sounded almost like a sob.

"He-he's my uncle Chris."

"Your uncle?"

"Ye-yes, Christopher Dunbar. He's my father's brother."

"Is he trying to kill you?" Slocum asked.

Ellie shook her head. "No. I don't know."

She started to tremble then, and Slocum put his arms around her. She was shaking like a leaf in a windstorm. Whatever was going on with her, Slocum knew that she was suddenly very frightened.

"It's all right, Ellie," Slocum said. "He can't hurt you now."

"It's not that. I haven't seen my uncle in years. I had almost forgotten about him. But today, I recognized the man on the buckskin horse. And I started shaking then because I had him in my sights and was about to pull the trigger."

"Who?"

"My father. That's why I recognized the horse. It's my father's and today, I saw him. John, I-I don't know what to say. None of this makes sense."

"Do you know who the third man is?" Slocum asked.

Ellie shook her head. "I didn't get a good look at him, but I probably wouldn't know him anyway. But that was definitely my father who was trying to kill us."

"Why would your father try to kill you, Ellie?"

"I don't know. Maybe he doesn't know it's me. I haven't seen him in a long time. Maybe he's forgotten what I look like."

"Maybe he wasn't trying to kill you," Slocum said.

"Huh?"

"Maybe your father was trying to kidnap you."

Ellie grew thoughtful for several moments. She looked down at the dead face of her uncle, shuddered, and then turned away. Slocum wondered if he had struck a nerve, a long-buried nerve.

"No, my father wouldn't do that. I really can't explain any of this. But I do know that my stepfather hated my father, and my father hated Ben's father. Maybe my father was settling an old grudge when he killed Mr. Travers."

"But if that's all that it was," Slocum said, "he's done that. Your father wants more than that. Is it the silver? The silver mine?"

"I hate to say this about my father, John, but yes, he might be after finding out where Mr. Travers has his mine and how rich it is."

"You asked me yesterday if I was an outlaw," Slocum said. "Was that because your father is?"

She turned and glared at Slocum, clenching and un-
clenching her fists. But her expression softened, and she
let out a long deep sigh. "Yes, my father was, is, an outlaw. He never cared much how he got his money, but our
mother did, and that's what caused all the trouble between
them, I guess. My father's a thief, a robber, and now, I
guess, he's a murderer, too."

"That's not your fault," Slocum said. "We don't pick
our folks, you know."

"I feel badly about Ben's father getting killed, John,
and now that I know who did it, I feel even worse. How
can I ever face Ben and Bettilee again?"

"What your father does shouldn't come in the way of
their affection for you."

"I don't know. Bettilee will blame me. I'm sure of
that."

"We don't have to tell her who killed her father, Ellie.
And, we don't have to tell Ben, either."

"No, I suppose we don't," she said. "But if Ben and
Bettilee ever found out . . ."

"How do you feel about your father now, Ellie?"

"I'm surprised that he would do what he's done to us."

"But you didn't like your stepfather all that much, did
you?"

"I didn't dislike him. He was kind to me."

"Your father probably killed him. At the least, he was
responsible for Travers's death."

"Yes, I guess so. What are you getting at?"

"Well, I shot and killed your uncle, and I may have to
kill your father before this is over. How would you feel
about that?"

"It was self-defense with Uncle Chris."

"And it might be self-defense with your father, too. If

he comes at me again, shooting to kill, I'll have to put him down."

Ellie shuddered. "I don't want to think about things like that."

"It's something you're going to have to face," Slocum said.

"I guess I'd have to say my father brought it on himself. I don't want him to die, of course, but he's an outlaw. He knows the risks."

"Well, I hope it works out," Slocum said, "but your father seems pretty determined to kill us all and get his hands on what's in that wagon."

"If my father rode up right now and asked for what's in that strongbox, I'd just give it to him and tell him to go away. It's not worth anyone's life."

"Do you know what's in the strongbox?" Slocum asked.

"No. Not really. But I have a pretty good hunch that there's a map in there."

"Did you ever go to the Travers mine?"

"No."

"And so you don't know where it is, do you, Ellie?"

"No, I don't."

But Slocum wondered if she was telling the truth, or if she was even telling him all she knew. Dunbar certainly knew his daughter was in the wagon, yet he continued to attack it. Was he so cold-blooded that he would kill his own daughter just to get his hands on the Travers silver mine?

It sure as hell looked that way, but Slocum knew that one could not always tell what a person's intentions were. Dunbar was persistent, and he hadn't tried to talk to Ellie. Maybe he was hoping Ellie would turn on her half brother and help her father gain control of the mine. But so far, that hadn't happened.

"Do you want to bury your uncle?" Slocum asked. "Or just leave him where your father can find him?"

"I-I don't know. I don't care. Just leave him, I guess."

"I doubt if your father will come back for him."

"Then let the buzzards have him," Ellie said, a bitter, angry tone to her voice. "I don't care what happens to Uncle Chris."

"I'll collect his guns," Slocum said, "and meet you back at the wagon."

"All right."

"Keep an eye out." Slocum walked over to Chris Dunbar's body and knelt down to unbuckle his gun belt. "We're not out of the woods yet."

"I know," Ellie said and walked back to the wagon.

Slocum picked up the rifle and carried it with him back to the wagon, his thoughts raging with questions and possible solutions.

Ellie was already in the seat, her rifle across her lap.

"What are we going to do about Uncle Chris's horse?" she asked, pointing to the animal standing hipshot a couple of hundred yards ahead of them.

Before Slocum could answer, they both heard a loud whistle. The horse lifted its head and looked in the direction of the whistle.

The whistle sounded once more, and the horse took off at a lope, then broke into a gallop. It disappeared over the rise.

"Well, that takes care of that," Slocum said.

"That means my father is not very far up ahead of us."

"I know."

Slocum handed up Chris Dunbar's guns to Ellie. He

had made up his mind on what he was going to do.

"Ellie, I'm going to saddle up my horse and ride ahead of the wagon. You'll drive it. I won't be far away, but I want to make sure your father doesn't jump us again."

"What about Ben?"

"We'll have to look at him when we stop for the night. If we're all in the wagon, we'll be sitting ducks for another ambush."

"I guess you're right," she said.

Slocum quickly saddled up the horse he had borrowed, slipped his rifle in its scabbard and mounted up. He rode up to the front of the wagon. Ellie had just emerged from inside and was back sitting on the seat.

"Ben's asleep," she said.

"Give me a head start of a hundred yards and then bring on the wagon," Slocum said.

"All right."

Slocum pulled his rifle out of the scabbard, pushed more cartridges into the magazine until it was full, and then rode off, staying well to the right of the trail. He topped the rise and started looking for Dunbar and the other man. And he knew where to find him. All he had to do was follow the tracks of Chris Dunbar's horse. They would lead him straight to Ellie's father.

In the distance, Slocum saw the two riders. They were leading the horse with the empty saddle.

And they were headed into rocky country that would afford them plenty of concealment.

Slocum kicked the horse in the flanks and put the horse into a ground-eating gait.

"One against two," he muttered. "Not bad odds."

# 9

Slocum rode well ahead of the wagon, but kept it in view. He knew that Dunbar and the other man could circle around and come up from behind. But for now, they were still in sight on the main road to Taos.

The country grew more rugged, with rocky outcroppings, deep draws, and wide ravines and the mountains to his right. Plenty of places for a man to hide, he knew, plenty of good places for another ambush.

An hour later, he lost all sight of Dunbar and he slowed his horse to a walk. He knew he dared not venture too far ahead of Ellie and the wagon, but if they didn't continue to make time, they'd never reach Taos. They still had Raton Pass to cross and that would probably be the most dangerous part of the journey.

Slocum left the road and started following the tracks through rough country dotted with cactus and rocky outcroppings. When he finally rode back to the road, he knew the men were way ahead of him, probably on their way to the pass or some place where they could have the advantage in an ambush. It was late afternoon when he slowed down and started to look for Ellie and the wagon.

Sunset was catching up to Slocum and casting long shadows across the land when he finally spotted the wagon. It was off the road and not moving and, for a moment, Slocum felt his heart fall. As he rode closer, his rifle at the ready, he saw Ellie slumped over, leaning against one of the wagon wheels.

"What's wrong, Ellie?"

When she looked up at him, Slocum could see that she had been crying. Her face was streaked with tears, and her eyes were red and slightly swollen.

"Oh, John," she wailed, "it's just impossible."

Slocum swung down out of the saddle and walked over to Ellie. He tied the reins to the wheel and knelt down beside her.

"What's impossible?"

"One of the horses is lame, so I had to stop. Then Ben called out for me, and I went back to tend to him. He's still got a high fever, and when I gave him water, he threw it right back up. I think he's in a lot of pain. I gave him some more of your whiskey and that quieted him down some. I just feel like everything's going wrong."

"Which horse is lame?" Slocum asked.

"That one," she said, pointing to the horse on the left.

"Let's take a look at Ben, and then I'll check both horses."

"All right." She stood up and sighed. "I'm glad you're back, John. I got to thinking something might have happened to you. This is the worst day of my life."

"If it is, then you have a happy life to look forward to," he said.

Slocum bent over Ben and looked at the wound in his

leg. He felt something twist in his gut as he saw that there were bluish streaks running up Ben's leg. The wound was suppurating and beginning to smell bad.

"What do you think, John?" Ellie asked.

"We'll just have to see," he said, unwilling to add to Ellie's despair. But it was bad for Ben. He most certainly was developing gangrene and the poison was advancing rapidly through his bloodstream. He cleaned the wound while Ben screamed in pain and poured more whiskey into it. But he knew it was a waste of good Kentucky bourbon. That was just not going to heal up.

"He's not doing well, is he?" Ellie asked.

"Not too well, Ellie," Slocum admitted.

"Isn't there anything we can do for Ben?"

"He needs a doctor, and I don't know if we can get him to Taos in time to save that leg."

"So, he'll be a cripple," she said, the tears welling up in her eyes once again.

"Maybe. Maybe not." Slocum didn't have the heart to tell her that it was very likely that Ben would die in the next few hours, or at least in a day or two. Ellie was near a state of hysteria, and he wasn't sure just how strong she was after all the blows that had been dealt her on this journey.

"Keep feeding him whiskey for his pain and try to get him to keep down some water," Slocum said. "That'll help."

"Where are you going?" she asked.

"To take a look at that lead horse. I won't ride off again today."

"Bless you, John," Ellie breathed.

Slocum grinned. It had been a long time since anyone had said that to him.

Outside the wagon, Slocum untied his horse and retied the reins to the back of the wagon on one of the struts that held up the canvas. He then went to the lame horse and picked up each foot in turn, expecting the worst. He started with the hind legs and then went to the right front. The shoes were on solid, and he could find nothing wrong with the muscles or tendons. But on the left front hoof, he found the reason why the horse had gone lame.

When he lifted the hoof, he saw a small, sharply pointed pebble that had slipped in under the shoe and was digging into the tender part of the horse's hoof. He worked the pebble loose and then used the butt of his pistol to pound the nail in tighter. He led the team a few yards to see how the horse performed.

The horse limped for a couple of steps and then the lameness disappeared. Slocum heaved a sigh of relief.

He looked at the afternoon sky and saw that the sun was already falling over the mountains and would soon set. He found a place where they might camp in safety and led the team over to a clump of trees on a flat place hemmed in by boulders and wind-stunted junipers growing out of the rocks.

Ellie peered out at him as he was unsaddling his horse.

"Are we staying here for the night?" she asked.

"Yes. Maybe we can get an early start in the morning."

"Can we have a fire, so I can cook something? Maybe I can get Ben to eat if he smells food."

"Yes, I think so. I don't expect your father to ride back here looking for us. Likely, he's found a place up ahead where he can wait for us."

"You think he'll come after us again?"

"I'd bet money on it," Slocum said, and he saw Ellie's

face darken with worry. But she held back the tears this time.

Slocum prepared a fire pit so that the flames would be below ground and then gathered firewood while Ellie broke out the foodstuffs for the evening meal. She cut up dried potatoes and some green beans, sliced off chunks of salted cured beef while Slocum built a fire. Ellie filled a pot with water and placed it on a rock in the center of the fire. She then put a skillet at the edge of the fire and dropped a dollop of grease in the pan. Then she added the beef and began stirring it so that it would brown and soften.

Slocum watched her with interest, knowing she was fighting off the sadness that engulfed her. She had already lost a stepfather, an uncle, and might soon lose a half brother and her own father. Slocum marveled at her bravery under the weight of all this grief.

As for Ben, Slocum had seen men even younger than he die a painful death from gangrene after being wounded in battle. The Civil War had claimed far too many good lives and left a lot of good men maimed and crippled for life. He had lost his own father and brother to the war between the states, and there was still an emptiness inside him from their deaths and his mother's.

But he had also seen some men overcome worse wounds and fight so valiantly against infection that they healed up, baffling the army surgeons and the nurses. So, he was not going to give up on Ben Travers. Not yet. The young man was in good health and might rally yet. Still, there was poison in the young man's blood, and it was racing towards his heart and brain like a prairie fire.

Slocum walked around to see how secure their campsite was. He looked at the fire from all angles and decided that the flames were low enough not to be seen from any distance. The smell of the food brought him back to the campfire where Ellie was stirring the pot of stew, the skillet lying on the ground, already cleaned with grit and waiting to be put away.

"Supper's ready," she said, setting out pewter plates, forks and knives. "I'm going to see if I can get Ben to eat some of this."

"I can wait," Slocum said.

Ellie dished up a small portion in a plate and carried it over to the wagon. Slocum sat by the fire, but he did not look directly at it. He watched the night spread its dark cloak across the land and listened intently for any alien sound.

Ellie returned in a few minutes, shaking her head.

"I couldn't get Ben to eat anything. I did spoon some broth into his mouth, but he didn't swallow it."

"You can try again later," Slocum said. "Maybe the taste of the broth will stir his appetite."

"I truly hope so, John."

Ellie folded her legs and sat down, dished up a plate of stew for Slocum and handed it to him. Then she ladled some on a plate for herself.

"Ben looks really bad," Ellie said, after taking a few bites of the food.

"Fevers are worse at night."

"It's not just the fever. He looks like he's giving up."

"He seems to be a strong young man, Ellie. Don't go looking for trouble."

"Is that what I'm doing, John?"

"Worry does no good unless you can act on it. In this case, we've done all we can for Ben. The rest is up to him."

"I guess you're right. How's the food?"

Slocum grinned. "It tastes wonderful. Jerky and hardtack can only take a man so far."

Ellie laughed.

"It's good to see you laugh. You've been under quite a strain."

"Yes, I suppose I have. But so have you. Are the horses all right?"

"Yes. The lead horse had a rock in its shoe. I took it out."

"I'm grateful and glad it wasn't something worse."

Slocum said nothing. He finished eating and dug out a cheroot, lit it from the fire.

"I don't need the fire anymore," Ellie said. "Shall I put it out?"

"Yes. No use drawing any more attention to ourselves."

He walked away then and looked at the horses, checked their hobbles, saw to it that they had grass enough for the night. He sat down, leaned his back against a flat rock. He drew on the cheroot and then blew the smoke out into the air, watched it hang there, then disappear in wisps. After a while, Ellie walked over and sat down beside him.

"A penny for your thoughts," she said.

"I was wondering why your father picked on the Traverses. Does he carry a grudge?"

"You know, John Slocum, you're a pretty smart man. You surprise me all the time."

"You mean I have a big curiosity."

"No, you're smart. Yes, my father hated Mr. Travers. There was bad blood between them."

"How so?"

"My stepfather testified against my father years ago. My father had robbed the store where Mr. Travers worked, and they threw my father in jail. He broke out, but when they took him away, he threatened Mr. Travers and said that someday he'd make him pay."

"That explains a lot," Slocum said.

"And I think my father was jealous that his wife married Mr. Travers."

"He left your mother, though, didn't he?"

"Yes, he did, but I think he always thought he'd come back someday. And she'd still be single and waiting for him."

"I don't understand men like that," Slocum said.

"What do you mean?"

"First of all, I've never been jealous or envious of any man. But I've seen jealousy destroy many a marriage and partnership."

"And what else?"

"Some men can't leave the past behind. They still try to live in it when it's already gone."

"I never thought of it that way," she said.

"It's simple, really. What's finished is finished. We can't live in the past, and we can't live in the future, because it's not here yet. The only life we can live is what's here and now, and I've come to believe that it demands our full attention if we're going to get through it."

"You sound like a philosopher," she said.

"No. I guess I've just ridden too many trails in my life."

"And this is another one for you. One you didn't ask for."

"Sometimes, Ellie, those are the ones that are the most interesting. And those are the ones we learn the most from."

"Are you thinking about tomorrow?" she asked, letting out a sigh.

"No. I'll think about tomorrow when I get there."

She laughed and then leaned over and hugged Slocum. She kissed him and whispered into his ear.

"Let's think about tonight, John," she said. "After all, it's already here."

"How right you are, Ellie," Slocum said and took her into his arms.

High up in the mountains, he heard a timber wolf howl and when he looked up, the stars had filled the sky, all twinkling with a far cold light.

# 10

Slocum wondered, the next day, how much more about her father Ellie wasn't telling him. The more he knew, the more questions he had. How did Jesse Dunbar know that Travers would be coming back from Pueblo, heading for Taos at just the right time? Why jump Travers when he did? Why didn't he kill him in Pueblo? Or Taos?

As Slocum hitched up the team, he mulled over these and other questions, but he would not express them to Ellie. Still, she was a puzzle to him. He wondered why Travers had brought her along on the trip to Pueblo. Was it because he didn't trust her?

And why did Travers leave Bettilee behind? All by herself? Did Bettilee and Ellie not get along? This was a most curious family, Slocum decided, and Dunbar might not be the only enemy he would have to face between here and Taos.

Ellie, despite his intimacies with her, remained a mystery. He was sure that she was holding many secrets and the fact that Ben himself did not trust her, told him a great

deal. For some good reason, Ben had not wanted to en-
trust Ellie with the map in the strongbox, and it was obvious that Ben's father did not completely trust Ellie
either. He had not shown her the mine nor confided in
her, and now he was dead and Ben was most surely dying.

All those thoughts ragged Slocum the rest of the day
as he drove the wagon toward Taos, with Ellie in the back
taking care of Ben, trying to get him to drink and eat and
trying to bring his raging fever down.

Slocum now kept the black saddled during the day, and
he tied the lead rope close to the front seat so that he
could mount the horse if needed—either to escape an ambush or to take the attack to Dunbar if he struck again. It
was slow and awkward going, but Slocum wanted to be
ready for anything.

The land stretched out and the road wound through it
with very little to command Slocum's attention. He saw
only a small herd of wild horses far out on the plain and
a few antelope grazing well out of rifle range.

He did not stop for lunch, but Ellie brought him some
of the stew that was left over and he filled his belly as he
continued to watch, not only the seemingly endless road
ahead, but also all that was around him.

By late afternoon, he could feel his nerves twanging. It
was like waiting for the other shoe to fall. He knew Dunbar and his henchman were out there somewhere, somewhere up ahead, but he didn't know where or when they
might attack again.

Slocum figured they were making just about twenty
miles a day, and the days were long. By the time they
started the climb up to cross through Raton Pass, he knew
his nerves were stretched taut as a banjo string.

Something was wrong, but he couldn't put his finger

on it. Ellie had turned distant on him, and Ben drifted in and out of delirium. But somehow, the young man was hanging on, despite all odds. They made dry camp late at night, and Slocum saw to it that they were back on the road long before sunup. Ellie complained, but not very much, and he thought that was unusual.

Later, Slocum would wonder if he had let himself become too complacent. There was something lulling and hypnotic about riding on that wagon all day. He found himself wanting to nod off and caught himself doing just that several times that last fateful day when he hoped to clear the pass before nightfall.

When it happened, Slocum was not in full command of his senses. He heard Ben call out his name, and then when Ben called again, his cry was suddenly cut off. Slocum pulled the wagon to a halt and set the brake.

That's when Dunbar and his crony rode up on him seemingly from out of nowhere. Slocum reached for his rifle and was about to cock it when he heard a noise from the back of the wagon. He turned just in time to see Ellie swing the shovel with all her might.

Slocum tried to lift up an arm to ward off the blow, but it was too late. The shovel smashed him square in the side of the head and he saw billions of sparkling stars flash in his head. Just then, he heard a shot and felt something hit him square in the belly. He was gripped with an immense pain and then everything went dark. He felt himself falling and heard voices that sounded like people speaking under water.

"Did you get the map, Ellie?"

"Yes, Daddy, I got it. But it's only half of the map."

"Bettilee's probably got the other half. Come on, get on Chris's horse, and let's light a shuck."

"What about Slocum here?"

"He's done for. I hit him square in the belly. He'll die slow, but he'll die."

"Ben's near dead now."

"Come on, shake a leg."

And then, Slocum heard Ellie scramble from the wagon and a few seconds later, he heard the pounding of hoofbeats. Then he fell into a pitch black pit as his head began to throb.

Slocum had no idea when he awoke, but it was still light out. When he looked up at the sun, it was starting to descend in the west, so he knew he had been out for at least an hour.

"Slocum," someone called, and as Slocum sat up, he realized it was Ben, still alive inside the wagon. "Slocum, come here," Ben said.

Quickly, Slocum collected his senses. His head ached as if someone was hammering it with a ten-pound maul, but he saw that the black was still saddled and tied to the wagon and his rifle lay on the ground. He crawled inside the wagon to see why Ben was calling him.

"Ben. I'm here."

"She put a gag in my mouth."

Slocum saw the piece of cloth that Ben had evidently spit out. It was lying next to his head. He also saw that the strongbox was open. Ellie hadn't bothered to close it.

"You've been shot, Slocum," Ben rasped. He was staring at Slocum's belly.

Slocum looked down at his midsection and saw the blood soaking through his shirt. He touched his hand there and it came away crimson. The touch brought pain to him and he gritted his teeth.

"I think Jesse Dunbar shot me when he rode up," Slocum said.

"I heard him brag about it before he left," Ben said. "Looks like you got a hole in you, Slocum. Maybe we're both going to die here."

"Hold on," Slocum said and began to unbutton his bloody shirt. He pulled his shirt up, exposing his belly, which was covered with blood spatters.

Then he reached down and touched the handle of his hideout pistol, a .32 Colt revolver. He pulled the pistol free of his waistband and examined it. One of the wooden grips was shattered. The lead ball had struck him there, sheared off splinters of wood that pierced Slocum's skin. The ball had broken up as it went through the frame and cracked the other wooden grip.

"Looks like this little Colt saved my life," Slocum said. He began picking splinters out of his stomach. He was badly bruised where the bullet had shattered the grips and smashed them against his flesh. But it had stopped the lead ball from penetrating his stomach and possibly ending his life.

Ben watched Slocum in fascination, his feverish eyes following each move as Slocum picked the splinters out of his stomach and washed the wounds.

"You were damned lucky, Slocum," Ben said.

"I know. I can get new grips for the .32 Colt. Now, let's see how you are doing. Did Ellie hurt you?

"No, but she got the key to the strongbox out of my pocket."

"I see it's open. Did she get the map?"

"Yes, damn her. But it won't do her any good."

"Why not?" Slocum asked.

"First of all, it's only half the map. Bettilee has the other half."

"They can figure that out, Ben."

"Even if they do, that's not all they need. Slocum, I have another copy of the half map they took in my left boot. Take it. And this locket around my neck."

"I'll do that when the time comes. If it comes," Slocum said.

"There-there's something else I've got to tell you."

"I'm listening, Ben."

"Do you know what an overlay is?"

"A map overlay?"

"Yes."

"I know what it is," Slocum said.

"When you put the two pieces of the map together, you'll still need an overlay to tell where our mine is."

"And who has the overlay?" Slocum asked.

"There are three of them, all very small."

"And?"

"They're behind Bettilee's picture in the locket I wear, the one I want you to take and show Bettilee."

"I don't even know where you live, Ben."

"The directions to our home are with the other half of the map in my boot. You won't have any trouble. The way to our house is clearly marked on the road. We live just north of Taos, five miles off the road."

"All right," Slocum said. The pain in his abdomen was fierce and he winced, tried to shut it out of his mind. But at least he was whole, which was more than he could say about Ben. "Can you eat something, Ben? Can you drink some water?"

"My leg is screaming with pain, Slocum. I don't have

any appetite, and it makes me sick to my stomach to think of drinking any water."

"I don't know how long you can last," Slocum said. "Do you want to continue the journey to Taos?"

"Yes. I've got the canteen here, and if I get hungry, I'll let you know."

"I wish there was something I could do for you, son."

"You've already done enough, Slocum. Let's get going."

"All right. Hang on, will you? I want you to ride this out. Drink some whiskey if the pain gets too bad."

"I will." Ben patted the bottle next to him. It was three quarters empty. Slocum's mouth watered just looking at it, but he could wait. Ben might need every bit of what was left and more.

"Let me look at that leg again," Slocum said.

"It stinks like hell."

"I know." Slocum pulled the sheet off of Ben and looked at the wound. It was ghastly, and there were blue streaks running up Ben's leg, a sure sign of gangrene. The hole that he had cauterized was now larger and the flesh inside had turned black from mortification.

"I wish you could cut it off, Slocum."

"I could do that, but you'd bleed to death in about two minutes."

"At this point, I wouldn't care. I've never felt pain like this. It's all over. It's in my bones, my brain, my mouth, my gut."

"It might be time for you to pray if you believe in such. Make your peace with your maker before you go."

"How long do I have?"

"I don't know. Maybe the infection will just stop, and you'll pull out of this."

"You don't believe that for a damned minute, Slocum."

"I believe that anything can happen if a man wants it to bad enough."

"Where do you get that idea?"

"I've seen men with worse wounds pull through. They said they had some little spark inside them that just wouldn't go out."

"What's that spark, do you think?"

"I think it's just a powerful will to live. No matter what. If you have that, you've got the spark, and it takes a mighty powerful wind to blow it out."

Ben's face took on a peaceful cast just then, as if he was mulling over his destiny or wondering if he had that spark of life that would keep him alive. Slocum kept silent, watching him.

"I'll try," Ben said, finally. "Before you get this wagon going, there's something I've been meaning to tell you. I couldn't talk about it when Ellie was still here."

"What's that?" Slocum asked.

"I think Ellie murdered my father."

"What makes you think that?"

"When you got shot a while ago, I listened real good to the sound of that rifle."

"And?"

"When my pa was shot, the sound of the rifle was different, and a lot closer. When Ellie was shooting before at those men, her rifle had the same sound."

"So, she was in this all along," Slocum said.

Tears welled up in Ben's eyes, and he nodded, his head bobbing up and down. Slocum grabbed one of his hands and squeezed it.

"It's too late to worry about that now," Slocum said. "You can't change what happened."

"I know," Ben said. "It's just that I've been such a fool. And Ellie betrayed us all. Even you."

"I know," Slocum said. "She's a dangerous damsel, that's for sure."

Ben closed his eyes, and Slocum saw a tremor roll through his flesh as if the young man was gripped with a pain so terrible, he didn't have the energy to scream.

# 11

Ben Travers hovered in that empty, desolate realm between life and death as Slocum rolled the wagon south toward Taos through ancient country that looked, at times, like the ruins of a vast city with its rock spires and bleak landscape dotted with Spanish bayonets, cholla, prickly pear cactus, and boulders that had rolled down from the foothills of the mountains.

Slocum could hear Ben every so often, moaning, snoring, struggling to breathe as the dust roiled up beneath the wagon and filtered in under the canvas. He knew that Ben could not have long to live and wondered now if perhaps Ellie had been the one to shoot him in the leg. But, no, that didn't make sense. It did make sense that she had shot Ben's father, though. Slocum wondered how such a beautiful face could hide such a cold black heart. Ellie had proven her treachery, however, and he had no doubt that she was a murderess. Perhaps, he thought, outlaw blood ran in her family, and she had been born to commit dark deeds.

Slocum drove well into the night, stopping only to tend to Ben and wait for the moon to rise before pushing on. He was careful to rest the horses often and grain them. He knew he was pushing them hard and didn't want them to founder in the next day's heat. There was plenty of water on the wagon, which was a blessing, since there was none to be had on that long, hard road south.

Slocum dozed, letting the horses find their way in the darkness, waking only long enough to see that they were still on the road. The horses moved at a brisk walk, not quite a trot, but stepped lively at an untiring pace, and so Slocum's luck held through the long night and into the next day. To stay awake, he smoked a cheroot and forced himself to keep an eye on the glow at the end of the cigar and to shake the ash off.

When Slocum halted to water and grain the horses, he checked on the young man and poured cool water on a cloth and rubbed his face and neck and chest. He forced some water into Ben's mouth and drank large amounts himself to saturate his muscles with moisture as the Apache did to cross the hot deserts of the southern plains.

Slocum pushed on, eighty miles, ninety miles, a hundred, and then, another day of twenty miles, taxing him and the horses very nearly to their limits. And still Ben managed to stay alive, although his lips were cracked and his fever raged and the heat inside the covered wagon matched the heat of his fevered brow.

Slocum drove over Raton Pass and headed down the long slope toward Taos, checking the tracks of three horses on the road when he stopped, knowing it was Dunbar, Ellie, and the other rider because of the nick in one horse's shoe. He measured the age of the tracks and knew they were less than a day ahead of him. He figured they stopped during the night to sleep while he and the team plodded on in the nocturnal coolness, like sleepwalkers in slow motion.

The gangrene was slowly eating up Ben's flesh like some ravenous animal, and he fought against the poison in his blood like some doomed gladiator of old losing the fight with lions in a Roman arena. He drifted in and out of consciousness and reason, unable to separate dream from reality. When Slocum gave him water, he drank, swallowing the few drops that managed to flow past his mouth, his throat as parched as if he had been abandoned on a desert. It broke Slocum's heart to see a man suffer as Ben was suffering, but time was his enemy, and he could not drive the horses any faster in the heat nor in the cool of night. They, and he, were exhausted, and by the end of their journey, the team was beginning to lose its spirit.

As the Sangre de Cristo range, with its snowcapped peaks, rose up from the deserted plain on Slocum's right, he knew he was drawing near to Taos, and he began to see Indians with their *carretas*, their two-wheeled carts, and lean, rangy dogs, ribs showing, appear out of nowhere, scavenging the land for scraps of food or trying to run down a sick rabbit.

Slocum figured he had less than twenty miles to go in order to reach the Travers's place. He could not see Taos in the distance, but he knew that he must be less than forty, perhaps less than thirty, miles from the town itself. He was looking now for the turnoff to the Travers's place according to the directions Ben had given him a few days before. He wondered if Ben would be alive when he rode in with the wagon.

He had lost the tracks of Dunbar in the maze of tracks

now covering the road. And, for the past few hours, he had passed traffic moving north, small caravans pulling wagons loaded with trade goods, men and women carrying furniture to new homes on unclaimed land in Colorado and Wyoming. Some folks waved to him, others turned their heads away at the smell of death emanating from the wagon.

Slocum came to a road and was surprised to see a post with names on boards cut like arrows, and one of them bore the name of Travers, pointing to his left. He noted the place and kept on going, slapping the traces to get the horses moving at a faster pace. If Ben was still alive, he wanted to get him to a doctor as fast as possible.

As he drew up on the outskirts of Taos, Slocum slowed the wagon and waved to the first Mexican he saw. The man stopped as Slocum hauled in on the reins.

"*A donde esta' un medico?*" Slocum asked.

The man thought for a moment, then pointed down the road. "*Vaya dos calles y vuelta a la izquierda. En el centro del calle hay una casa con un medico.*"

Slocum thanked the man and drove the two blocks, turned left and there, in the center of the street, on his right, in an adobe dwelling, was a door with a sign reading MEDICO. He pulled the wagon to a stop and set the brake, jumped down.

He ran into the doctor's office and saw people crammed in there like apples in a crate, all huddled together on crude benches. He strode past them and entered another room. There he saw a man sitting on a wooden table with his shirt off. A man, obviously a doctor, had been examining him. The doctor looked up in surprise, spoke to Slocum in Spanish.

"What is it you want, sir?"

"I have a very sick man outside in a wagon," Slocum said in Spanish. "He has the gangrene. Can you help me carry him in here? He's dying."

"I do not know if I can help him."

"You can cut off the leg if that will save the man."

"I will see," the doctor said. To the man on the table, he said: "Come with me, Pedro. Grab that pallet by the wall and bring it."

Outside, Slocum dropped the tailgate and pulled Ben toward the rear of the wagon. The doctor and Pedro came up. Pedro set the pallet down on the ground. Slocum and Pedro lifted Ben and set him on the pallet, which was like a primitive stretcher.

Pedro wrinkled his nose when he smelled the infection that was eating Ben alive. The doctor sniffed and told Pedro to hurry. Slocum and Pedro carried Ben into the doctor's office, put him on a table in the back room.

"Do you speak English?" Slocum asked.

"Yes. I am Doctor Aguirre, and you are?"

"The name's Slocum. John Slocum."

"What happened to this man? It appears that someone cauterized his wound, but some time ago."

"He was shot. I burned the wound closed, but it opened up again."

Aguirre bent over and examined Ben's leg. He took a knife and cut away the remaining cloth of his trousers and exposed the entire leg, clear to the hip.

"I will have to cut off this leg, Mr. Slocum."

"I figured that. Can you save his life?"

"I do not know. Is he your brother?"

"No, he's not any relation to me. He's just a man I met on the trail."

"You have done well to keep him alive this long. But

he is near death, I think. Can you pay for the surgery?"

"Yes," Slocum said, without hesitation. "How much?"

"Have you a hundred pesos?"

Slocum gave him some bills. The doctor counted them and gave some of the money back.

"This is enough for now. Come back later. I make no promises."

"I understand, Doctor. Do what you can. I'll be back sometime. Today or tomorrow."

"No later than tomorrow, Mr. Slocum."

Pedro stood there, pinching his nose to stop the smell.

"There's something I have to do before I go, Doctor," Slocum said. "Just bear with me."

As the doctor and Pedro watched, Slocum removed the locket from around Ben's neck. Then he removed Ben's boots and fished in the bottom for the map. He found the map and stuck it in his pocket.

"You are robbing this man?" Aguirre asked.

"No, these are things he asked me to take from him should he die. His name's Ben Travers."

"But he is not dead."

"It's a long story, Doctor. I am not robbing him."

"Very well. I trust you, Mr. Slocum."

Slocum touched a hand to his hat and left the room. He strode through the office and went outside where he asked a passerby where he might find a stable. The man told him, and Slocum climbed up into the wagon and drove four blocks to the stables. It was open, and he parked the wagon and walked inside. A Mexican met him inside.

"Can you keep this wagon and board those two horses? I'm riding the other one."

"Two pesos a day for the horses, a peso a day for the wagon."

Slocum peeled off a five dollar bill, and the man's eyes widened.

"Will that cover it?"

"Yes, for two or three days, I think."

"I'll be back. I'll take the black horse and leave the rig here with you."

"I will keep them for you."

The man's name was Nestor Roxas, and he seemed honest enough. His hands were gnarled from hard work and the weather, and his stables were neatly kept. Slocum rode away, feeling he had accomplished a great deal in a short time.

Now, he had a long ride to the Travers's place. He hoped Bettilee would be there, but he knew that she might have company.

Dangerous company.

# 12

As soon as Slocum rode away from the stables, which he
noted had no sign out front, he felt he was being followed.
The streets were crowded with men and women strolling
in and out of small shops, with carts carrying crates full
of chickens and fresh vegetables, with boys herding goats
and pigs, a lot of men on horseback, and a few carriages.
The street was lined with trees that were in full foliage,
so he could not see very far in either direction.

Taos was, he knew, a city of commerce, with a diverse
population. While he had put the whiskey bottle in his
saddlebags before he left the stables, he knew there were
only a few swallows left. And he had developed a powerful thirst after all the days he'd spent on the road going
without even a taste of the good Kentucky bourbon that
he so dearly cherished. He knew there had to be a cantina
somewhere nearby, and he started looking for one while
trying to shake off the feeling that someone was following
him, someone he did not know on sight.

Slocum turned on another street, which was even more

crowded than the other one, and then, hoping to shake off whoever was following him, he turned on still another street, stepping the horse up to a trot while trying to avoid all the foot traffic on the avenue. Finally, he saw a cantina ahead and rode toward it, glancing over his shoulder all the time.

He dismounted and tied up at a hitching post cemented into the adobe bricks outside. He looked up at the sign. COPA DE ORO, the sign read. Slocum went inside, squinting to adjust to the darkness. The place was small, but busy. There were a few tables where men were sitting, talking, drinks in front of them.

Slocum found a place at the far end of the bar where he could keep an eye on the door. A couple of Mexican women glanced at him, smiled. The men gave him one look and turned their heads the other way.

The bartender, a short, stocky man with a huge handlebar moustache strode over with a bar towel and wiped a spot in front of Slocum.

In Spanish, the man said, "What do you wish? A cup?"

"Do you have whiskey?" Slocum asked, in Spanish. "From Kentucky?"

The man shook his head. "I have whiskey. It is American. That is all I know."

"What is it called?"

The man turned around, reached down, and pulled out a bottle that had a little dust on it. He wiped it clear and showed it to Slocum.

"Old Taylor," Slocum said, smiling. And, in English, said, "That is good Kentucky bourbon. I will have a glass."

"At your service," the bartender said, reaching for a glass. He poured it half full and left the bottle beside it. "You are American."

"Yes."

"The Americans, they do not come in here much. I bought this whiskey from an American who came from the States."

"You speak good English," Slocum said.

"In Taos and in Santa Fe, we speak the English and the Spanish. It is good for the business."

Slocum put a silver dollar on the counter. The bartender picked it up, put it between his teeth, and bit it. Then he went to the cash drawer and made change. He put the change, in pesos, on the counter.

Slocum swallowed the whiskey slow, letting it slide down his throat like warm honey. He drew in a deep breath and let the whiskey do its work. He smiled.

"The whiskey, she is good, no?"

"It is very good whiskey," Slocum said, keeping his gaze on the front batwing doors. He heard some wheels squeak outside and then come to a stop.

"You are expecting someone?" the barkeep asked.

"Maybe. Why?"

"You look at the door, and there is no one there."

"Habit," Slocum said.

"And you carry the rifle and wear the big *pistola*."

"That is true. I did not want to leave the rifle outside with my horse. Someone might steal it."

"You are right. Someone would surely steal it. It would be a—how do you say it?—a temptation."

"Yes. It might be."

"I hope you will not use the rifle on the one you are waiting for. That is why I say these things."

"The rifle is leaning against the bar by my feet," Slocum said. "I do not plan to use it on anyone who comes in here for a drink."

The bartender seemed relieved. He smiled and moved away. But he kept one eye on Slocum as he waited on other patrons, the women and other men at the bar. One of the men sitting at a table lifted his hand and one of the girls at the bar spoke to the bartender who poured mescal in two glasses. The girl took the drinks over to the table and brought back some bills which she laid on the counter. She looked longingly at Slocum and smiled.

Slocum turned away from her, not wanting to encourage her to come over and talk. But he knew she was available if he needed company. Right now, he had too many other things on his mind. He finished the glass of whiskey and pulled out a cheroot, lit it. He knew he should be riding back out to the main road from Pueblo to Taos and then head for the Travers's place, but he knew damned well somebody was following him, and he wanted to find out who, and why.

Slocum had learned a long time ago to trust his instincts. It was something he had learned when he rode with Quantrill, something he had learned at the same time he learned to use a six-shooter. During the war, the hunter was often the hunted, as well, and when he was riding with the Raiders, often through the thick woods of the Ozarks, where it was difficult to see very far ahead or behind, it was often necessary to trust what he liked to call "another eye." That eye was the one within, the one that could see beyond what was apparent. Some called it a sixth sense, others instinct, and still others said it was like "following your hunches." Well, he felt that way now, and that instinct, that inner eye, had never failed him, not in the war, in bloody Kansas, nor since.

And now that inner eye told him he was being followed. Of course, this was not something he could see with his naked eye. But he could feel it as surely as always if someone in a room was looking at his back. He couldn't see the person, but, invariably, when he turned around, he would find that person who was staring at him.

He did not want to get drunk, so he drank the second shot of whiskey slow, savoring its flavor, its heady aroma, and the warmth it brought to his vitals. Gradually, the muscles in his shoulders and legs began to relax, and he realized how much on edge he must have been for the past several days.

The bartender drifted his way, and Slocum realized he had to relieve himself.

"*Tengo que miar?*" he asked the bartender.

"*Afuera. Hay un puerto alla'. Detras.*" He pointed to a back door.

"I'll be right back," Slocum said, picking up his rifle. He walked to the back door and down a hallway to another door, then outside, to an alley. There, he relieved himself, letting out a sigh. He went back inside the cantina and sat down where he had left his drink. He leaned his rifle against the bar and gazed around the room.

There were more patrons at the bar, men he had not seen before, and he stared at them intently, studying each face. He recognized none of them. He turned his head to look at the tables, and that's when he heard a sound he never expected.

Slocum's blood froze as he heard the metallic click of a hammer cocking. Then he felt something cold and hard against his temple.

"You reach for that Winchester, mister, and I'll splatter your brains all over that wall back of you."

Slocum didn't move.

But he knew he had made a serious mistake and might possibly pay for it with his life.

Time stood still for a long moment, and he waited for the man to squeeze the trigger. He wondered if he would even hear the explosion before his lights went out.

# 13

Slocum weighed his options. He wondered if he had time to duck and pile drive a fist into the gut of the man who held the pistol to his head. As if reading his thoughts, the man with the pistol pressed even harder and spoke in a harsh whisper.

"Don't even think about trying anything, mister. Just get up from that barstool real slow and walk out the front door. I'll be right behind you with this .44 on full cock, and my trigger finger itching like a son of a bitch."

"You're calling the turn," Slocum said.

"And shut your damned mouth," the man said.

Slocum drew a breath and held it. Then he got up from his seat and stepped back. He moved around the bar, feeling the barrel of the pistol pressed into the small of his back. He heard the man pick up his rifle with his left hand. He still hadn't seen the man's face, but his brain was scrambling to figure out who in the hell had gotten the drop on him.

And something else.

How to get that pistol out of his back.

Slocum saw his chance when they approached the batwing doors. The man behind him prodded him to go outside, and the right hand door was the nearest. But just as Slocum lifted his hand to push on the right door, his left hand shot to the left door. It swung open, and he shot through. At the same time, he elbowed the right door back inward as hard as he could push.

Then everything seemed to happen at once. Slocum felt the door crash into the man holding the pistol to his back. Slocum spun to the right, shot his hand out and grabbed the pistol out of the man's right hand, which was doubled over at the wrist after the door had struck the barrel of the pistol. Slocum stepped back inside, snatched his rifle from the man's left hand. He grabbed it by the barrel and then swung it upward as the man staggered away. The stock caught the man in the side of the head and knocked him off balance. Slocum followed up his advantage and barreled forward, shifting his grip on the rifle so that he was holding it by the stock. Then he swung the barrel and struck the man in the face, knocking him to the floor. The man lay on his back, groggy from the last blow. Or so Slocum thought.

The man kicked a boot into Slocum's shin with great force. Slocum slumped almost to one knee as the man crabbed toward him, kicking with his other leg. The man's boot caught Slocum in his other leg, and he felt it go out from under him. The rifle slipped from Slocum's grasp and thunked onto the dirt floor. The men at the next table, rose from their chairs and melted into the more crowded part of the room.

Slocum still held on to the man's pistol, and he swung it at the man's head. But the blow missed, and the man leaped onto Slocum and grappled with him, both hands reaching for Slocum's throat.

Slocum wriggled out from under and closed his left fist. He brought it up and jabbed straight for the man's jaw, connecting just below the right cheekbone. Then Slocum scooted backward and tried to regain his footing.

The man swung a hard roundhouse right at Slocum. His fist glanced off Slocum's shoulder before cracking him in the mouth. Blood began to seep from one corner of Slocum's mouth as he fended off more blows from his attacker.

"I know you, you bastard," the man grunted, and he drove a pile driver left arm into Slocum's midsection, knocking the wind out of John. Slocum doubled over, but straightened out quickly as the man waded into him with both fists swinging like a windmill gone berserk.

Slocum slapped one of the man's forearms with the barrel of the pistol and then sidestepped and drove a left hand into the man's kidney from the side. The man grunted and expelled air. The blow spun him around, and he tottered on one leg for a few seconds.

That was all the time that Slocum needed to press his advantage. He grabbed the man by the shoulder with his left hand and turned him around until the two were facing each other. Then, Slocum feinted with the pistol. The man's eyes glanced upward at the pistol, and Slocum drove a boot into the man's groin, catching him square in the balls.

The man screamed in pain and crumpled into a knot of agony on the floor. Slocum walked up to him and pushed him backwards, hard, until the man lay sprawled on the dirt of the cantina, spread-eagled like some fallen scarecrow, flat on his back.

Slocum stepped in and pushed the man's pistol forward until the barrel rested flush between the man's eyes.

"Talk fast, or I'll blow your brains out before you have time to say a last prayer."

"God, d-don't shoot me, mister. I-I was only following orders. I-I didn't know it was you I was a-goin' up against or I'd never come in here. You are John Slocum, ain't ye?"

"What makes you think I am?" Slocum asked.

"You don't remember me, do you? And, I don't blame you much if you don't."

"Am I supposed to remember a sack of garbage like you?"

"I was at Gettysburg when you was fightin' alongside one of my kin, Tom Spence. He was my cousin. You and him was sharpshooters, remember?"

"I remember Tom was a crack shot."

"So was you, Slocum."

"You was mad as hell when Pickett made his charge and your brother Robert got killed. You took a Spencer off'n a bluecoat and put it to good use, I recollect."

"Where in hell were you?"

"I wasn't far away. I watched you and Tom cuttin' down them men in blue fast as you could load. Your gun barrels got so hot, you had to pour your canteens on the barrels. Then the damned Yankees started laying down grapeshot and all whatnot on you and I got the hell out."

"Ran, you mean?"

"We was ordered back up on Round Top."

"That was a long time ago," Slocum said. He looked around the room. The patrons were all frozen at their tables or standing in the back. But the bartender stood at the farthest end of the bar. He held onto a Greener, double-barreled, which lay across the bar.

Slocum's eyebrows arched in a querulous look. The bartender grinned and patted the shotgun.

Slocum nodded his thanks and turned his attention back to the man on the floor. "You said you were following orders when you came here," Slocum said.

"Yeah, like a dumb ass."

"Whose orders?"

"Some lady. She-she gave me two dollars to come in here and brace you."

"What lady? She have a name?"

"If she did, she never told me."

"What's your name?" Slocum asked.

"Cleve. Cleve Sutphen."

The man was obviously rattled, scared out of his wits. His eyes flared wide as if he had walked into a lightning bolt. He had a scraggly beard, seemed down on his luck from the looks of his worn and ragged clothes. Even the pistol was old and about as reliable as a Waterbury watch that had been dropped down five hundred feet of rocky cliff. It was an old Navy Remington converted from cap-lock to percussion. The firing pin was worn down to a nub, and the bluing had long since worn away from being handled by sweaty palms and sitting in a rotting leather holster.

"You're pathetic, Sutphen," Slocum said. "Some strange lady gives you two greenbacks to go up against somebody you don't even know. You're lucky I didn't blow a hole through your gut when I first saw you going down."

"I'm mighty grateful, Cap'n Slocum."

A sudden memory flashed across Slocum's mind. He

had been promoted to captain, after Gettysburg and then was assigned to General Price, which led him eventually to Quantrill. There was something in the tone of the man's voice when he called him *Cap'n* that made him remember the young soldier back at Round Top. But he still couldn't recall his real name.

"Did they call you *Short Britches*?" Slocum asked.

The man cracked a feeble smile and nodded.

"You remember me now, don't you, Cap'n?"

"I remember Short Britches and you sound like him, look a little like him, maybe."

"I've growed a lot since then. That nickname followed me from back home in Calhoun County, Georgia."

"I didn't know you back there," Slocum said.

"Nope, I was from the other side of the Alleghenies, same as Tom Spence."

Slocum was tired of reminiscing, and the clock was ticking. Everyone in the cantina was still frozen, waiting, he supposed, for him to put a bullet in Sutphen's brain so that they could get back to swilling their cheap tequila and mescal. He knew who Sutphen was now. Tom had talked about the Sutphen clan on the other side of the mountains, regaling all of them with strange tales of that backwoods bunch of no accounts. And here was Cleve Sutphen, the lowest of the low, hiring out to a strange woman for a couple of greenback dollars.

"Where is this lady who paid you to jump me?"

"I-I don't know. She was a-settin' in a buggy acrost the street, last I saw her. I seen her looking in here, not wantin' to be seen and I was curious. I think she was a-follerin' you before you came in the Copa here."

"What makes you think that?"

"I was acrost the street, me and Bob Rand, sippin' on

a bottle of mescal, and I seen you come in and then I seen this lady in the buggy come right up and jump out and run over here just after you came in."

"Get up, Sutphen. I want you to take me to this lady right now."

Sutphen gingerly rose to his feet and swayed there on unsteady legs for a long moment, seemingly still groggy from the beating at the hands of John Slocum. Slocum gestured with the converted Remington in his hand. As Sutphen started for the door, Slocum reached down and picked up his Winchester. He looked at the bartender and nodded his thanks. The bartender nodded back.

Slocum could almost hear a collective sigh of relief as he and Sutphen ambled toward the batwing doors. Slocum stayed well behind Sutphen, letting him go through first.

"If you run, Sutphen, I can shoot right through that door and you won't get five feet."

"I ain't goin' to run, Cap'n," Sutphen said, as he stepped through both batwing doors. Slocum came up right behind him, out into the street. A quick look showed him the buggy across the street.

The buggy was empty.

"Where is she?" Slocum asked.

Sutphen shrugged.

Just then, Slocum heard an ominous click and his heart sank down through his boots. Sutphen heard the sound, too, and turned around. Then, a slow grin washed across his face as he looked just past Slocum toward the outer wall of the cantina.

"Shoot him," Sutphen said, and Slocum braced himself for the shot he knew would come.

He had made another stupid mistake, he realized, and again, he was about to pay for it with his life.

# 14

Slocum held his breath, waiting for the shot that would surely end his life. He could sense that the person holding the gun on him was very near, too close to miss.

"Drop that pistol, mister. Just open your hand and let it drop to the ground. The rifle, too."

The hackles rose on the back of Slocum's neck as he slowly released his grip on Sutphen's pistol. He let out a breath, then laid the rifle down. A woman's voice. And there was nothing more dangerous than a woman with fire in her eye and a gun in her hand.

"Sutphen, pick it up and move away from that man."

"I know this man," Sutphen says.

"Well, I don't. I just know he stole a wagon from my father. And he's got some explaining to do before I take him to the *juzgado*."

"Yes'm," Sutphen said. "I don't know nothin' 'bout no wagon, but this man here is John Slocum. I served with him at Gettysburg. If you're a-goin' to kill him, you better shoot him in the back right now, because he's hell with a Colt and tricky as a sidewinder."

"I don't care if he's Ulysses S. Grant," the woman said. "Get your pistol and shoot him if I miss."

Sutphen gulped, but retrieved his pistol and backed well away from Slocum. He kept his pistol pointed at the woman's prisoner.

"Turn around, real slow," the woman said to Slocum. "And keep your hands way up high."

Slocum turned slowly and looked at the woman. His jaw fell open slightly, and he sucked in a breath.

She was beautiful, more beautiful than her picture, by far, and the simple dress she wore did not hide her ample curves, her fulsome breasts. But she held the pistol steady on him and her pretty blue eyes never blinked. Not once.

"What are you looking at?" she asked.

"You look much prettier in person than you do in your picture, Bettilee," Slocum said.

Bettilee Travers reacted as if he had slapped her in the face with a wet bar towel. She blanched and her lips quivered slightly.

"How do you know my name?"

"I didn't steal your pa's wagon," Slocum said. "I drove it down here with Ben dying in the back of it. I dropped him off at a medico's office and then put the wagon and horses up at the stables until I returned from your place."

"Ben? Is he all right?"

"He might not make it. Your father's dead. Ellie shot him."

"Ellie? Pa dead?"

For a moment, Slocum thought Bettilee might swoon. Her eyes closed for a second, and she swayed on her feet as if a sudden wind had sprung up and was threatening to topple her.

"It's a long story," Slocum said. "But I came upon them, Ben, your pa, and Ellie, when they were being attacked by Ellie's father and two other men."

"Jesse Dunbar?"

"Yes," Slocum said, and that's when Bettilee's knees turned to jelly, and she started to crumple. Slocum stepped toward her and caught her in his arms before she fell. Sutphen gestured with the pistol, but did not shoot. He could see what was happening. He just stood there and gawked.

"How do I know you're not just making this up?" Bettilee asked.

"Ben told me to take the locket he wore around his neck and show it to you. The one with your picture in it, Bettilee."

"That's my name. Where's the locket?"

"I have it. It's in my pocket. Want me to show it to you?"

"You just hold right still, Mr. Slocum. Get your hands up. Where is Ben now? Where did you take him?"

"I can take you there, the one near those stables. Doctor's name is Aguirre."

"I don't know him," she said.

"I have some other things for you, too, but I don't want to talk about it here. Too many big ears." Slocum shot a quick glance at Sutphen.

Bettilee hesitated. She looked at Sutphen, then back at Slocum as if trying to make up her mind what to do. Sutphen still held his pistol in his hand, and it was aimed straight at Slocum. It would be an easy shot. So, too, did

Bettilee have the drop on him, and his arms were tiring from holding them up in the air.

People on the street did not stop to see what was going on, but they did glance over at the strange sight of a man being held at gunpoint by a woman and a man, all gringos. Slocum wondered how long they could stay out here without a soldier or a member of the local constabulary stopping by to ask questions and see what was going on.

"Cleve, I think you can go on now. I paid you your two dollars."

"I think you might owe me a bit more, ma'am. Slocum was more trouble than I thought. He liked to have killed me."

"You better take Miss Travers's advice, Sutphen," Slocum said, his voice low and threaded with warning. "She paid you, and you accepted. That's it."

"I don't rightly think so, Cap'n."

Slocum looked directly at Sutphen. His eyes burned like hot coals. He glanced beyond him at the lone man sitting on a bench with a nearly empty bottle of mescal in his hand. Bob Rand wouldn't be much trouble in his condition, Slocum thought.

"If you shoot me, that'll likely be your last shot, Sutphen. If you miss, I'll drop you. If you hit me, Miss Travers will put your lights out real quick. Isn't that right, Bettilee?" Slocum turned to look at her.

Bettilee swung her pistol to bear on Sutphen. The meaning was obvious.

Sutphen swallowed hard and his Adam's apple bobbed up and down.

"Aw shoot," Sutphen said. "I reckon I don't want to open the ball with you, Cap'n Slocum. 'Sides, we both got out of the war alive, I reckon. No use messin' that up now."

"I'll be seeing you, Sutphen," Slocum said.

"Thank you for your help, Cleve," Bettilee said.

Sutphen holstered his pistol.

Slocum stooped over and picked up his rifle as Stuphen walked away to join his friend Rand at the mescal bottle.

"You said you were heading for my place, Mr. Slocum. Why?"

"Dunbar and Ellie, and one other that I know of, were heading there. Ellie stole one half of your father's map to his silver mine. You have the other half. I believe they mean to get it from you."

"Did Ben tell you about that, too?"

"Yes, and he had another copy in his boot. I have that with me, and some overlays."

"It seems we have a lot to talk about."

"I imagine Dunbar is waiting for you at your place right now, Bettilee."

"I want to see Ben. Will you take me to him?"

"Yes'm, I can do that. He may not be alive, though. He's got gangrene in his leg. Bad."

Bettilee shuddered. She looked as if she was about to cry. Then, she stiffened and stood up straight.

"Then, all the more reason to go and see Ben now," she said. "That's my buggy over there." She pointed.

"And that's my horse," Slocum said, nodding to his left.

"You can tie him to the buggy. Are you ready to go?"

"I'm ready. Just give me a minute."

Before he went after his horse, Slocum walked over to the bench where Sutphen and Rand were sitting. He looked at both men, as if in pity.

"Sutphen, I guess the war didn't teach you a damned thing."

"What do you mean, Cap'n?"

"You were ready to shoot me. For two measly dollars. If you think life's that cheap, I feel sorry for you."

"I wasn't goin' to shoot you, if'n I could help it, Cap'n."

"I think you were. Before I leave, I'll give you boys something to think about."

"What's that, Cap'n?"

"The answer to your misery is not in that bottle of mescal, and if you ever come at me with a gun in your hand again, I'll blow you to kingdom come."

"That a threat, Slocum?" Rand asked, speaking for the first time.

"Call it what you want, Rand. The same goes for you."

"Slocum," Rand said, "you just don't know how cheap life is in Taos. Yours included."

"You won't think it's so cheap if you find yourself at the business end of a Colt .44."

With that, Slocum turned on his heel and walked back across the street to get his horse.

Slocum had seen such buggies before, back home in Georgia, but he had never ridden in one. He had always admired the kind of horses the rich people, those who owned the plantations and the factories, used to pull them, high-stepping thoroughbreds with sleek sorrel or coal black coats. This buggy that Bettilee drove was not so fine, but it had good springs and was comfortable, and she handled the single-horse shay like a professional, seldom using the whip, or her voice, as they wound back through the dusty streets of Taos to Dr. Aguirre's.

Slocum noticed that Bettilee had been crying while he

had retrieved his horse and tied the reins to the buggy.

"You're crying," he said. "Over Ben?"

"Ben and my father. I still can't believe he's dead."

"We buried him in a place where you can find his grave and bring him back home if you want to, Bettilee."

"Yes, I think I'd want to do that. Did-did he suffer? I mean . . ."

"I don't think so. Ellie shot him at close range. I think he died quick."

Bettilee dabbed at her eyes, but the tears continued to flow.

"I suppose I'm glad of that. But our pa was such a good man. He was secretive, but he said there was so much silver ore in his mine that we would never have to worry about money again."

"But you don't know where the mine is."

"No. He and Ben wouldn't let me know. Pa said it would be dangerous. He wanted to do one more assay far away from either Taos or Santa Fe. That's why he went to Pueblo."

"It cost him his life. Was the mine worth that?"

"I-I don't know. It was important to Pa. And to Ben, too. It was something they did on their own, and they were proud of their accomplishment."

"That mine might cost Ben his life, too. And yours."

"Mine?" She turned and looked at Slocum.

"Dunbar and his henchman. And Ellie. They'll stop at nothing to get their hands on the complete map."

"I would never let them do such a thing. They should not profit from their misdeeds. From murder."

"I agree with you," Slocum said.

When they pulled up in front of the doctor's office, Bettilee set the brake, and she and Slocum climbed out.

At the door, Bettilee hesitated. Then her shoulders shook as she bowed her head. She started crying again. Slocum put an arm around her shoulder.

"I-I don't know if I can go in there," she said. "I-I'm afraid of what I might find."

"You have to face it, Bettilee. Sooner or later."

"I know," she said. "I know. I just . . ."

And then she broke down, and the tears flowed. Slocum squeezed her with his arm and waited out the flood of grief and worry that gripped her.

He felt sorry for Bettilee. She had lost her father and was probably going to lose her brother, as well. She was young and beautiful, and if Ben died, she'd be all alone.

A wave of tenderness washed over him and his jaw tightened as he thought of the treachery Ellie and Jesse Dunbar had wreaked on the Travers family.

All in the name of greed.

## 15

When Bettilee stopped crying, Slocum patted her gently on the back and ushered her inside the doctor's office. She clutched the small carpetbag she carried close to her chest as if for both support and comfort. The waiting room was empty and, at first, they could not hear a sound. It was as if the place was deserted.

Then, they both heard low moans coming from beyond the waiting room door. Slocum took Bettilee's arm and led her across the waiting room. He opened the door without knocking and found the place where he had left Ben in Dr. Aguirre's care. The room was brightly lit.

"Hello, Dr. Aguirre. I brought with me the patient's sister."

"Come in. Be quiet," Aguirre said.

There was a damp cloth over Ben's forehead. A nurse stood next to him on the other side of the operating table. She was holding a small metal bowl in her hands. There was a strong smell of medicines and what Slocum knew was ether. That was probably what was in the bowl the nurse was holding.

Slocum had to restrain Bettilee from rushing to her brother's side. As he held her, he could feel her body shaking, her skin quivering under her blouse. Her hands were trembling as she fought back the fear that clasped her heart in a fist.

The doctor was working furiously on Ben's leg. He was cutting away dead flesh. Slocum could see that the wound had been cleaned and disinfected. The smell of gangrene was no longer present, overpowered by the unguents and medicants that the doctor had obviously administered while Slocum had been gone.

"I am trying to save the leg," Aguirre said, as if reading Slocum's thoughts. "But it may have to be removed, perhaps just above the knee."

"How's he doing, Dr. Aguirre?" Slocum asked.

The doctor looked up at the nurse and nodded. "Alicia," he said.

Alicia bent over and put her ear close to Ben's mouth. Then she straightened up, looked at the doctor and nodded.

"He's still breathing," Aguirre said.

Bettilee heaved a sigh of relief.

"Maybe we should wait outside," Slocum suggested.

Bettilee shook her head. "No, I want to stay here." She looked at the doctor and asked, "Doctor, can't I help, or at least put my hand on my brother's forehead?"

"It would be better if you did not come too close. Your brother is very infected, and I do not want him to get more infected."

"I see," Bettilee said, but there was a slight bitterness to her tone, and Slocum knew that she did not see at all.

She wanted to comfort Ben, and she was being deprived of that nurturing and touching.

Ben did not look good. His face was drawn, and he looked haggard and weak. The nurse kept dabbing the sweat off his forehead with a towel, and every so often, when Ben stirred, she'd give him a little whiff of ether from the cloth soaking in the bowl she held in her hands.

Bettilee was doing her best not to cry as she watched Dr. Aguirre work. The wound was a hideous thing, and with the dead and mortifying flesh scraped away, she could see bone and raw flesh. Every so often, the doctor soaked up blood in a cheesecloth and threw it down into a bucket below the operating table. Finally, he finished and covered the entire wound with a yellowish salve and then put compresses on it. Then he wound cloth around the bandages and tied them off neatly. When he looked up, his face was covered with a thin sheen of sweat.

"Come," Aguirre said, "we can talk in the waiting room. Alicia, let him come back awake but give him the laudanum if he has the pain."

"Yes, Doctor," she said.

"I'll wash up and meet you in the waiting room," Aguirre told Slocum and Bettilee. "Have yourselves a seat, eh?"

Slocum nodded. He and Bettilee went out into the waiting room. He looked out through the window and saw that the sun was falling away to the west. Shadows were beginning to build in the street outside. It would be dark as soon as the sun fell below the skyline of the Sangre de Cristo range. It would be dark and there were a lot of things he and Bettilee had yet to do. If she wanted to do them.

Dr. Aguirre met with them a few moments later. His

hands looked clean, were well scrubbed and he had changed shirts and no longer wore the apron that had been stained with Ben's blood.

Aguirre sat down. "I think your brother, Ben—is that his name?—he is very sick and very weak. But his heart is good, and he is strong in spirit, I think."

"Can you tell me what his chances are, Dr. Aguirre?" Bettilee asked.

Aguirre, a thin, wiry man in his late thirties, with a thin moustache and long sideburns, seemed to turn older in that moment when he pondered Bettilee's question. His bright, brown eyes seemed to darken for a second or two as he looked off in the unfathomable distance beyond Bettilee and Slocum. He lifted his hands up from his lap as if to examine them in the light and then heaved a heavy sigh. He cleared his throat before he spoke.

"These hands," Aguirre said, "can only do so much for such a wound as your brother Ben has. I think we must look beyond my hands to the hands of another."

The doctor looked up at the ceiling, then dropped his head.

"You mean . . ." Bettilee began.

"I mean, sometimes there are ailments that medicine cannot cure. Sometimes, a doctor must rely on other forces to help him with his healing. And sometimes, these hands of mine do not heal at all unless I touch them together like this and pray." The doctor pressed his hands together in an attitude of prayer.

Slocum knew what Aguirre was talking about. He had seen what seemed to be miracles on the battlefield, and he had heard surgeons discussing among themselves how a soldier, given up for dead, found some hidden strength to defy death and recover without any physical assistance from a physician. Some cases defied explanation.

"Are you asking me to pray for my brother, Doctor?"

"I am praying for him," Aguirre said.

"So, do you think I ought to stay with him?" she asked. "Be of some comfort if he . . . if he . . ."

"I do not think your brother will die right away. Not tonight. He needs rest, and he will be given medicines by mouth and soups that will give him back some strength. If you stay here and do not sleep, you will be of no help tomorrow when he may need to see you. He is tired. Very tired. He will sleep, and he will awake tomorrow. He will not have much pain. Alicia will watch him and give him the medicine for pain, and I will have another nurse come in at midnight and take your brother under her care. Do not worry."

"But I am worried," Bettilee said.

The doctor reached over and patted her shoulder. "I know, but it will do you no good to worry. You must have faith and trust. Your brother is in God's hands now."

"Can I see him? Talk to him?"

"It would be better if you did not disturb him. He cannot hear you. He is very deep in sleep. Come back tomorrow. In the morning. I will be here early."

"I think he's right, Bettilee," Slocum said. "There's nothing more that you and I can do. It's getting dark now, and you need food and rest."

Bettlee sighed and looked at Slocum. "I know you're right," she said. "In my heart, I know you're right, both you and Dr. Aguirre. But I feel there must be something I can do for Ben."

"There is not," Aguirre said. "Now, go. Come back in the morning. Eat. Sleep."

The doctor smiled. Slocum rose to his feet and took

Bettilee's hand. He touched a hand to his hat in farewell to the doctor and led Bettilee outside. She clutched her carpetbag to her tightly as if holding on to a life raft.

"What do you want to do now, Bettilee?" Slocum asked. "You can't go home. Do you have a place to stay in Taos tonight?"

"Why can't I go home?" she asked.

"Because I have a feeling, a very strong feeling, that the Dunbars are waiting for you. They've already murdered your father and would not blink an eye at killing you, as well."

"I see," she said, walking toward the buggy. "What are you going to do?"

"I was meaning to ride out to your place alone and look it over. See if I can't take them out, one by one."

"You'd shoot Ellie? A woman?"

Slocum didn't even hesitate. "If she drew on me, I would be a fool not to shoot her. I might not try to kill her, but put her down and disarm her. She's a dangerous woman. A deadly woman."

"Yes, she is. I know."

Slocum waited for her to explain, but she climbed up into the buggy and set her handbag down beside her. She picked up the reins and looked at Slocum.

"Are you coming with me?" she asked.

"Where are you going?"

"I'm going to a hotel. I'm going to bathe and eat supper. You're welcome to join me. Besides, Jesse and Ellie can't do anything without the other half of my father's map. And the overlays."

"They are probably tearing your house up right now looking for that other half of the map. They don't know about the overlays."

Bettilee smiled.

"They can look all they want for the other half of the map," she said. "I keep it with me all the time."

"You have the map with you? Now?"

She reached over and patted her bag. "Yes, right in here. Right underneath my pistol, Mr. Slocum."

Slocum let out a low whistle and dug into his pocket, searching for a cheroot. He found one, the last he had on him, and took it out. He struck a lucifer and lighted it, drew in the fresh smoke.

"I'll ride with you to the hotel," he said. "It seems we still have a lot to talk about."

"Yes, that's a good idea," she said. "And we can make plans after we look at the entire map and the overlays."

"What do you have in mind?" he asked.

"I'll tell you over supper. Besides, I want to see Ben first thing in the morning. It's a long ride out to my place, and I doubt if you could find it in the dark."

"You'd be surprised at what I can find in the dark," Slocum said, climbing into the buggy.

"I'm counting on it," she said, smiling. "I don't like to be alone. I've been that way for too long. How about you?"

Slocum cleared his throat.

"I don't like to sleep alone," he said, "now that you mention it."

"That's what I mean," she said and snapped the reins up and down. They crackled on the back of the horse as she pulled off the brake and the buggy lurched into motion.

"That's exactly what I mean, Mr. Slocum."

# 16

Cleve Sutphen watched the buggy pull away from the doctor's office with that woman, Bettilee Travers, and Captain John Slocum in it, pulling that black horse along with it.

"Seems to me, Cleve, you'd want to stay away from that Slocum feller."

Bob Rand wasn't drunk, but he was warm all over, and there was some fuzz on his tongue. And that two dollars Cleve had in his pocket was sure as hell burning a hole in his own pocket. He wanted another drink.

"Slocum's up to something. He's pretty smart, and I hear he's a wanted man."

"Not by me, he ain't," Rand said.

"I know he kilt a judge back in Calhoun County, Georgia, after the war, and there's a price on his head."

"Well, we're sure a hell of a long way from Georgia."

"Don't you know who that woman is with Slocum?"

Rand shook his head. And he licked his dry lips, hoping Sutphen would notice that they were plumb out of mescal.

"She's old Ethan Travers's kid. I didn't put it together right off, but once't I got to thinkin' about it, I 'membered what I heard about Travers."

"I ain't never heard about Travers or his kid," Rand said.

"You don't listen real good, Bob. Travers was haulin' raw ore to Santa Fe and had a assay done here in Taos afore that, and talk was that he had found a rich vein of silver. Then, he starts sneakin' around, disappearin' for days and weeks at a time, and then he hauls some ore up north, to Pueblo, I hear, and some folks are mighty anxious to know how that assayed out and just where in hell Travers has got him that silver mine."

"What has that got to do with Slocum?" Rand asked.

"Well, that Miss Travers said Slocum stole her pa's wagon, stuck it in a stable while he ambles off to that cantina. She hires me to jump him, only I don't know it's Slocum she's chasin'."

"So?"

"So, I figure Slocum must be in with Ethan Travers or maybe Ethan told him about the mine and where it is. Anyway, I got real curious when them two, Miss Travers and Slocum, all of a sudden ride off together, and there ain't no sign of Ethan Travers. And they go to that medico yonder and then come out and ride off together."

"You got a curious mind, Cleve, that's more tangled up than a nest of young snakes. I don't foller you at all."

"We're going to go over to that *clinic* yonder and find out who in hell they got in there that Miss Travers is so curious about. Could be old Ethan Travers hisself."

"Well, shit fire, Cleve, I don't see where that gets us anyplace. And my throat is as parched as a widder's pussy. I badly need some liquid refreshment."

"You keep your damn pants on, Bob. We'll get us a drink directly."

Rand grinned and slapped his knee.

"What're you agonna do, Cleve?"

"I want you to foller Slocum and that Travers gal, then come back and get me here when they light someplace. I'm goin' to walk over to that medico's office and see who he's got in there."

The buggy was just turning the corner when Rand mounted his horse and galloped up the street after it. Sutphen walked briskly across the street and entered Aguirre's office. When he came out a few minutes later, he went back to where his horse was tied and built himself a cigarette, sat down under a laurel tree and smoked slow, watching the sun disappear over the Sangre de Cristo range, plunging the street into shadows.

Two more cigarettes later, Sutphen got to his feet as he saw Bob Rand approaching on horseback. He stubbed out the cigarette under his boot heel and walked out into the street to halt Rand.

"What did you find out, Bob?" Sutphen asked.

"First, what did you find out across the street, Cleve?"

"Well, ain't you the damned smarty-face? I found out Travers's kid is over there, dyin' of a gunshot wound. The little gal there said the doc was going to saw off the kid's leg pretty soon."

"So, what does that give us, Cleve?"

"It means Miss Bettilee Travers ain't goin' to leave town real quick. Now, where'd she and Slocum light down?"

Rand chuckled. "Oh, they went to that *posada* over near them stables she was talkin' about."

"What *posada's* that, damn it?"

"It's called Posada de Luna. I lit down and watched them through the window. There was some plants growin' just past it, but I seen 'em real clear."

"Damn you, Bob, spit it out, will you? What in hell did you see 'em do?"

"Well, they both checked in at the desk and then they went into the dinin' room. Oh, Slocum put his horse up at that stable just down the street first. Then they both come back to the hotel in the buggy."

"You done real good, Bob. I'll get my horse."

"What about that drink, Cleve?"

"We'll get that drink and a whole lot more. You just keep your damned britches on, Bob."

After Sutphen had mounted his horse and rode up alongside Rand, he spoke to his friend. "Follow me," he said.

"Where we goin', Cleve?"

"To get us some damned pesos, that's where."

Rand grinned wide and fell in behind Sutphen who rode at a leisurely place down the *calle*, building another smoke as he sat easy in the saddle.

Sutphen and Rand pulled up in front of the stables, tied their horses to hitch rings. Sutphen started to walk inside. There was a lantern lit and light shone through the wide front doors.

"Whatcha goin' to do, Cleve?" Rand asked.

"Just don't say nothin', Bob. Leave this to me."

"Whatever you say, Cleve."

Inside, a young Mexican man was cleaning some of the stalls with a pitchfork. He was separating the horse apples from the hay and putting them into a wooden wheelbarrow.

"You speak English?" Sutphen asked.

"Yes, I speak the English," the young man said.

"I'm here to pick up that wagon and my horses."

"Oh, yes. You come back early. Rodrigo, he say you might come. The wagon is out back. I will get the horses."

"Hitch 'em up for me, will you?"

"I will do this," the young man said.

Rand looked at Sutphen. Sutphen just grinned as the stable boy went to first one stall, then the other, and led out the two horses Slocum had brought in with the Travers wagon.

In a few minutes, Sutphen and Rand were riding out of the stables. Outside, Sutphen halted the wagon and climbed down.

"Just follow with the wagon, Bob. I'll lead your horse."

"Where we goin'?"

"I know where I can sell this wagon and the horses for a pretty good price. We'll sleep in a good hotel tonight, maybe the Posada de Luna and have all the drinks and grub we want."

Rand grinned wide.

"Damn, Cleve, you sure as hell know how to treat a thirsty man."

"I'm just as thirsty as you are, Bob."

"After we sell the wagon and do all that, what then?"

"Why then, Bob, my friend, we're going to be like a shadder to old Cap'n Slocum and just see where he and that little lady leads us."

"You mean get us some silver?"

"I mean you and me, Bob, may be rich men real soon."

Bob grinned again, and the grin stayed stuck to his face as he followed Sutphen through the dim-lit streets of Taos.

# 17

Slocum handed Bettilee the locket he had taken from her brother, Ben. She took it, opened it, and tears filled her eyes.

"Thank you," she said. "I'm glad you waited until we had finished our supper. I'm just a big old crybaby."

"Inside, under your picture, Bettilee, are those overlays your father made."

"I don't know what overlays are," she said, her voice just above a whisper. She dabbed at her eyes with a corner of the napkin. The dining room was nearly empty, but there were a few patrons on the other side of the room. The waitress had disappeared after bringing them coffee and taking away their supper dishes.

Slocum looked at her in the glow of the candle on the table, and the tawny light from the oil lamps along the walls. She was truly a beautiful woman, but he sensed a sadness in her eyes and an edge to her that he had seen in others who had grown up on the frontier, who had survived the harsh conditions of overland travel and the

131

years absent from Eastern civilization. To him, such a look added charm and dignity to a woman, and Bettilee had both in abundance.

"Don't take your picture out here," Slocum said. "Too many eyes and ears."

Bettilee looked around the room. None of the patrons seemed to be paying any attention to either of them. Each was absorbed in the ritual of dining or its aftermath.

"Everyone here looks harmless to me," she said.

"Those overlays are probably very thin, and you could spill coffee on them, or they could get knocked off the table and ground underfoot. I have the other half of the map in my pocket, and if you have your half, we can do this in my room. Or yours."

"Our rooms adjoin each other," she said.

"That wasn't my doing, Bettilee."

She smiled. "No, it was mine. I feel safer with you in the room next to mine."

"That might be a false feeling of safety," he said.

"Why?"

"Doors," he said.

"Doors?"

"If you lock your door between our rooms it would take time to break it down. By that time you could be badly hurt, or worse."

Bettilee laughed. "So, you think my door should be unlocked."

"And, mine, too."

She laughed again.

"It's not important," he said. "Your room is your room."

"And yours is yours. Is that right?"

Slocum smiled.

"Unless it was just one big room with an unlocked door in between. For coming and going."

"Are you trying to seduce me, Mr. Slocum?"

"No, ma'am. I don't do that kind of work."

"Oh, so you consider seducing a lady a chore, some kind of work?"

"I didn't mean it that way."

"I know you didn't." She smiled at Slocum. "Maybe I was trying to seduce *you*. Or, at least, trying to find out if I *could* seduce you."

"Do you *want* to seduce me?"

She laughed.

"Do you *want* to be seduced? Do you do that kind of work?"

"Sometimes."

"Well, this is a very romantic inn. And I don't have a beau. Are you married?"

"No, ma'am. Would it make any difference?"

"It might. I have morals you know."

"I know. I didn't mean it that way."

"How did you mean it, John?" She reached across the table and put her hand on his.

"I guess I wondered how far you would go with a man you hardly know."

She kept her hand on his and looked into his shadowed eyes, eyes that were not directly in the light.

"Sometimes a woman can tell about a man. Even the first time she meets him."

"And can you tell about me, Bettilee?"

She smiled. It was a warm smile, and it melted something in his heart.

"I think so. You don't look like a philanderer, or a wolf in sheep's clothing. I'd say you were a man with his own high standards. That you treat any woman like a lady, even if she's not."

Slocum said nothing, but he felt Bettilee's foot nudge against his leg and begin rubbing it. The expression on her face did not change as she gazed into his eyes, a slight trickle of a smile making her lips quiver.

"I think we'd better go upstairs," she said. "I'm dying to put the two halves of my father's map together and see how those overlays work."

"Can you read a map?" he asked.

"My father taught both me and Ben how to read maps. He thought they were important and used maps to find his way out here to Taos."

"All right. I'll pay the bill, and we'll go upstairs." Slocum looked around the room again. Their waitress was still out of sight. He snapped his fingers.

"What about that *mozo* you sent out before we came in here?" Bettilee asked. "Shouldn't he be back now?"

"I don't know," Slocum said. "But here comes our waitress."

The waitress came up and presented Slocum with the bill. He paid her and gave her a tip. She thanked him and was leaving when the boy came in from the lobby of the inn carrying a cloth sack.

"Here's the boy now," Slocum said.

The boy handed Slocum the sack. He smiled.

"What did you have him bring you, John?" Bettilee asked.

"Some bourbon and two dozen cheroots. There's also a bottle of Mexican wine in here. I thought you might like a taste after supper."

The boy gave Slocum his change, and Slocum counted

out five silver pesos and placed them in the boy's palm. The boy thanked him, bowed, and left.

"How thoughtful of you," she said. "The perfect end to an almost perfect evening."

"The evening is yet young," Slocum said, rising from his chair. He walked around and pulled out Bettilee's chair so that she could get up.

"I'm glad you said that," she said, smiling, as she picked up her carpetbag. "You've helped lessen my worries about Ben."

"Worry doesn't help much," he said. "In fact, worry can make the problem seem a lot bigger."

Bettilee put her arm inside Slocum's and walked with him outside of the dining room and into the lobby. They were about to start up the stairs to their rooms when Slocum turned suddenly as something outside the inn caught his eye.

"Go upstairs and get my rifle," he told Bettilee. "Hurry. Take this sack up to my room. Here's my key."

"Why? What's wrong?" Bettilee grabbed the sack from Slocum and took the key to his room.

"I just saw your friend Cleve Sutphen ride by, leading another horse. And right behind him, driving your wagon was none other than his friend Bob Rand."

"Wait for me," she called, as she raced up the stairs.

"They're heading west," Slocum said, spreading his black frock coat wide and drawing his pistol. "I think I can stop them."

Slocum raced out of the hotel and out onto the street. He looked to his right and saw the wagon rumbling away from him. It was not going very fast, and he thought he could catch up to it if he ran fast enough.

He had his pistol out, but he didn't have a shot at Rand,

who was in front of the covered part of the wagon. Ahead of the wagon he saw Sutphen pause before turning the corner. But when Sutphen glanced up the street, he reined to a halt and held up his hand to stop Rand and the wagon.

It would be a long shot, Slocum thought, as he ran down the street, trying to catch up with the stolen wagon. His only worry now was whether or not Bettilee could catch up with him.

He damned sure was going to need that Winchester, unless he missed his guess.

And even as Slocum thought that, he saw Sutphen jerk a rifle from its scabbard. Now, Slocum thought with irony, he was racing straight into a .44 caliber bullet that might have his name on it.

# 18

Slocum saw Sutphen raise his rifle as the wagon skidded to a halt just before the street intersection. He ducked into the shadows, then crossed the street just as a rifle shot cracked like a whip. He heard a whizzing sound and saw the bullet plow a furrow in the street where he had been.

Now, he put the wagon between him and Sutphen and continued to run toward Rand, hoping to come up on his blind side.

Luckily, Slocum thought, the street was deserted at that time of night when most folks were taking their suppers or filling up the cantinas. He did not have to worry about innocent citizens getting shot. Only himself.

Slocum heard the clatter of iron horseshoes as Sutphen apparently turned his horse to head it back to the other side of the wagon. Slocum's heart pounded in his chest as he raced to beat Sutphen to the side of the wagon where both were headed.

The wagon stayed motionless and Slocum dashed in a zigzag pattern to come up directly behind the tailgate.

That's when he saw Sutphen's horse come into view on his left side. Slocum ducked and ran around to the right, then to the front of the wagon.

"Rand," Slocum said, throwing his Colt .45 down on the man "set the brake and climb out of the wagon on this side."

"You go to hell, Slocum."

Slocum cocked the single-action six-gun. To his surprise, Rand balled himself up into a crouch and dove over the other side of the wagon. A second later, he ducked as a rifle shot sent a bullet just over his head. Out of the corner of his eye he saw Sutphen atop his horse, a smoking rifle in his hands.

"I'm coming," Bettilee shouted from down the street.

Slocum's heart sank. Had he drawn her into a life-threatening situation by asking her to bring him his rifle? She was running right into danger, and he was in a tight spot himself.

"Go back," Slocum yelled. "Go back, Bettilee."

"I've got you, Slocum," Sutphen said, riding around the horses in harness at the front of the wagon. "Bob, you get your ass after that Travers woman."

Slocum ducked beneath the wagon. Somehow, he knew he had to eliminate himself as a clear target and stop Rand from shooting or capturing Bettilee. At the same time, he needed to get the drop on Sutphen. Atop that horse, with a rifle, he was a big threat.

Slocum could no longer see Bettilee, and he didn't know whether or not she had gone back to the inn or found a place of safety. As he hunched over and crossed to the other side of the wagon, he heard a noise nearby. In the darkness, it was difficult to see.

"He's under the wagon," Rand said.

Slocum saw movement in the direction Rand's voice had come from, so he squeezed off a quick shot. The Colt bucked in his hand and belched orange flame and burning sparks. The bullet whined as it caromed off something in the street and shot off into the ether. He heard what he thought was Rand scurrying away.

Slocum slipped out from under the wagon and ducked low as he came up to the wagon tongue. Beyond, he saw the legs of the horse Sutphen was riding. The horse was trying to turn around in a circle and when Slocum saw its chest, he fired point-blank straight into it.

The horse reared as the bullet tore through its chest. Slocum hated to destroy good horseflesh, but he had no choice. As long as Sutphen was mounted, he had mobility and that mobility could cost Slocum his life, and, perhaps, Bettilee's as well.

The horse reared up and then collapsed as its hind legs turned rubbery, no longer able to support the animal's weight after its forequarters had buckled under the impact of the bullet. Slocum heard a body hit the street, and Sutphen let out a grunt as his butt hit the ground and the air rushed from his lungs.

"Damn you, Slocum. I paid thirty bucks for that horse," Sutphen gasped.

Slocum headed for the sound of Sutphen's voice, his pistol cocked. Slocum slid around the hind legs of the fallen horse. To his left, a pistol shot rang out, and he heard the bullet slam into the dirt a few inches behind his feet. He drew in his legs in case Rand fired again.

Slocum saw a flash of orange flame off to his left and a shadowy figure go into a crouch and take aim again. He spun to his right and leaped straight at the fallen horse. That act probably saved his life, because Sutphen fired off another shot from his rifle at the same instant.

Slocum hugged the ground, then scrabbled around to the right of the dead horse. He saw Sutphen get to his feet so that he could try for a better shot.

In that instant, Slocum saw his chance to rush Sutphen while he was still off guard. He got to his feet and ran straight for Sutphen, who was halfway up and had not yet levered another round into the chamber of his rifle. Sutphen's face registered a look of surprise as Slocum hurtled toward him.

Sutphen tried to swing his rifle around as he stood full upright, and, at the same time, clear the empty shell in the chamber and reload. Slocum smashed into Sutphen, knocking the rifle from his hands. Sutphen staggered sideways under the force of Slocum's attack, and Slocum clubbed him in the side of his head with the barrel of his Colt.

Sutphen crumpled and fell to his knees. Slocum kicked him in the chest with the heel of his boot. Sutphen fell backwards, flat on his back. Slocum knelt down and shoved the barrel of his pistol in Sutphen's face.

"You move, Sutphen, and your face turns to jelly."

Then Slocum heard footsteps off to his left. He turned in time to see Bettilee running in the direction where he had last seen Rand shooting his pistol at him.

"Get down," Slocum yelled at Bettilee.

Sutphen started to laugh. It began as a chuckle in his throat and then burst out in a dry cackle.

"Shut up, Sutphen," Slocum hissed, pushing the barrel of his pistol hard against Sutphen's temple for emphasis.

"Looks like you might lose your girl, Cap'n," Sutphen said.

"Don't bet it on, Sutphen."

Bettilee melted into the shadows and Slocum could no longer see her. He was surprised that she had taken the initiative and continued on down the street when he had told her to stay back. He saw that she was carrying his Winchester, though, and hoped she knew how to use it.

While Slocum was looking off to his left, Sutphen was not idle. His hand slid down toward the butt of his pistol, and when Slocum turned around, Sutphen had his hand around the grip.

Sutphen was fast. Before Slocum could register all of it in his mind, Sutphen raised one arm and knocked Slocum's hand away, the hand with the pistol. With the other hand, Sutphen drew his own weapon and swung the barrel of his pistol at Slocum's head.

Slocum felt the iron strike him just above his right temple, and, for a moment, there was blackness, then a cascade of sparkling lights flashing in his brain. He staggered off balance from the force of the blow, and then Sutphen was on him like a cat pouncing on a mouse.

Swinging his fist and his pistol, Sutphen rained hard blows on Slocum's face and chest. There was a fury in his attack that sounded a warning in Slocum's mind. He knew that if he didn't get away from Sutphen, he would go down, and Sutphen would kill him.

Slocum tried to bring his gun hand up to fire point-blank at Sutphen, but Sutphen, anticipating this move, smashed downward with his pistol, striking Slocum's forearm with stunning force. Slocum felt the pain shoot up his arm and down into his wrist and jangle his fingers, which still gripped his pistol tightly.

Then he heard the ominous cocking of Sutphen's pistol and, out of the corner of his eye, he saw the six-gun swinging toward him as if to bring the barrel in line with a spot right between Slocum's eyes.

Slocum knew, in that instant, that his life hung by a slender thread. In a split second, Sutphen would squeeze the trigger, and Slocum would turn into a corpse on a dark street in Taos, where nobody cared who lived or died.

# 19

In that eternity between life and death, Slocum summoned up every last ounce of strength and will to break free of Sutphen's grip on him and turn the tables on his would-be slayer. Despite the pain in his right forearm, despite the numbness in his fingers, he brought up his pistol in a furious thrust towards Sutphen's gun hand. At the same time, Slocum jerked his head as far to his left as he could and dug in his heels and pushed with his legs.

Sutphen was so sure of himself that he had not counted on Slocum's powerful resistance, nor his equally powerful will to live. Slocum squirmed to the side as Sutphen squeezed the trigger. The explosion deafened Slocum, but the bullet missed his head by a fraction of an inch, giving him time to plow his pistol into the side of Sutphen's head with a glancing blow.

Sutphen grunted in pain and fell away, allowing Slocum to scramble free and regain his footing. Slocum pounced on Sutphen in a fury, slashing with the barrel of his pistol. He cracked Sutphen on his left cheekbone, laying it open to the bone. Blood gushed out and streamed down Sutphen's face as he tried to bring up his pistol for another shot at Slocum.

Slocum stepped over Sutphen and stomped his boot down on Sutphen's wrist, crunching it into the dirt. Sutphen screamed as his gun hand opened and the pistol fell from his grip. Slocum kicked the pistol away with a quick slash of his boot, then brought down the butt of his pistol square on top of Sutphen's head, lacerating the scalp so that blood bubbled up from his skull and soaked through his crumpled hat.

"Enough," Sutphen gasped. "You win, Slocum. Don't hit me no more."

"I ought to blow your brains out, Sutphen."

"Then do it, Cap'n. I ain't got no more fight in me."

"We'll see about that," Slocum said, lifting Sutphen up off the ground with his left hand grasping his shirt front. Then he hauled off with his gun hand, smashing Sutphen on the tip of his chin with a tremendous force, only the knuckles striking the skin. But with the weight of the pistol in Slocum's hand, the blow was so powerful it jarred Sutphen into unconsciousness. He staggered backward, his eyes closed, and fell down, out cold.

"That should do it for you, Sutphen. Now, there really isn't any more fight in you."

Slocum, panting, picked up Sutphen's pistol and stuck it in his waistband. Then he walked over and retrieved Sutphen's rifle. He jacked the lever several times, ejecting all the cartridges, then threw the weapon down hard. It rattled when it hit the ground.

Turning, still panting for breath, Slocum raced to the side of the street beyond the wagon to see if he could help

Bettilee. He heard muffled sounds coming from a dark passageway between two buildings.

"Bettilee?" Slocum called.

Slocum listened intently for the slightest sound. He thought he heard muffled groans and turned his head so that his ear was facing the dark corridor between the two buildings.

That's when he heard a couple of quick footsteps right next to him. He began to turn toward the noise when something heavy slammed into his shoulder, nearly knocking him off his feet. He staggered back out into the street and tried to regain his footing.

The hunched over man charged into Slocum, hit him square in his gut with his head. He felt arms wrap around his hips in a tackle hold and then he was down on his back with someone breathing whiskey fumes into his face.

Slocum recognized Bob Rand as his attacker just before the man threw a roundhouse right that connected with Slocum's jaw, almost knocking him senseless. He struggled to maintain consciousness as Rand began to rain blows down on his head with both fists.

"I'll give you what for, Slocum, you bastard," Rand husked.

Slocum writhed and twisted to escape the fury of Rand's slashing attack. He brought up a knee and drove it into Rand's side, but it seemed to have little effect on the man. Rand stopped hitting him and, instead, tried to grasp Slocum's throat to choke the life out of him.

Slocum batted Rand's hands aside and moved his head and neck to escape strangulation. Rand bore down on him with powerful arms and hands, still trying for a stranglehold on Slocum's neck.

Slocum dropped his pistol well out of Rand's reach and

slipped both arms inside of Rand's, spreading them apart. He grabbed Rand by the shirt collar and pulled him over his head. Then he pushed upward, lifting Rand from his body. At the same time, Slocum brought a leg back and kicked upward at Rand's crotch. He felt his boot connect and heard Rand scream in pain.

Rand doubled over in agony and Slocum flipped him onto his back. Then he flopped atop him and drove a fist straight into Rand's mouth. He felt the squish as he mashed Rand's mouth into bloody pulp. Blood squirted from the crushed lips and streamed down both sides of Rand's mouth. Rand's eyes glazed over as he struggled to get out from under Slocum's crushing weight.

"If you've hurt Bettilee, Rand," Slocum breathed, "I'll break your neck. You might live, you bastard, but you'll never walk on two legs again."

"Damn your hide, Slocum," Rand spat.

That's when Slocum grabbed Rand by both ears and began slamming the back of his head down on the ground. Hard. He felt the fury building in him, building to a towering rage, a rage strong enough to kill Rand with his bare hands. All he could think about was Bettilee lying in the dark, dead or hurt, and Rand responsible for the black deed.

"John, stop."

Slocum felt a shiver rush up his spine. He stopped pounding Rand's head into the dirt and looked around. Bettilee was standing there, holding his Winchester.

"I'm all right," she said. "He knocked me out for a few minutes, but he didn't kill me."

"I ought to kill him," Slocum said.

"Is that what you are, Mr. Slocum? A killer of men?"

Slocum was surprised at the question, but it deserved

an answer. Not in detail, of course, but an answer that would satisfy her as well as him.

"Sometimes," he said.

"I meant by profession."

"No. I don't work at it."

He stood up, dusted himself off, and looked Bettilee in the eye.

"I'm glad," she said.

"What do you want me to do with these two? Put them in jail? Tie them up and put them behind one of these adobe buildings?"

"Just leave them like the trash they are," she said.

And Slocum was surprised again at her.

"I'll take the wagon and horses back to the stable and leave orders that only you or I can pick them up."

"I'll go with you," she said. "Then, perhaps, we can finish the business you and I have together."

"Yes," Slocum said, still looking into her eyes. And what he saw there was not only a promise, but a challenge.

Slocum reached into his pocket and fished for a cheroot. He drew it out and struck a match, lit it, drew deeply of the smoke, filling his lungs.

"That's the last cheroot I have with me," he said, a lazy curl of a smile on his lips.

"Luckily, I have the ones you sent the boy for in my room," she said.

"When you picked up my rifle, you didn't leave the sack there?"

"No," she said. "I opened the door between our rooms and put the sack on my bed."

"That was thoughtful, Bettilee."

"I thought so," she said.

She came close and squeezed Slocum's hand, then drew it close until it rested high up on her leg. "Shall we put up the wagon and the horses now?" she asked.

"I think that's a splendid idea, Bettilee."

In moments, they were driving the team back to the stables. Slocum drew on the cheroot while Bettilee sat next to him on the seat, her leg nestled next to his. She held his free hand and when she put her head on his shoulder, a sudden thought came to him.

"I know why you opened the door to your room before bringing my rifle to me," he said.

"You do?"

"It's a woman thing, I think."

"A woman thing?"

He leaned over and nuzzled his nose in her hair, sniffed deeply.

"Yes," he said. "You put on fresh perfume. I can smell it in your hair and behind your ears."

"You're a very observant man, John Slocum."

"And you're some kind of woman, Bettilee."

"Just wait," she said. "You don't know the half of it."

Her voice was a whisper, but he heard her clearly, and the perfume was strong in his nostrils, stronger than the scent of smoke from the cheroot.

"I can't wait," he said softly.

Bettilee squeezed his hand in total agreement.

# 20

Bettilee turned the lamp down low in her large room. She had opened the windows to let in the evening breeze, bathed with a damp towel and put on some rouge and perfume. She heard Slocum in his room next to hers. She could hear him rise from his chair and walk to the open door that separated their rooms. The lamp had been a predetermined signal.

From downstairs, Mexican music wafted through the window, a soft, soothing melody mellow with guitars and a violin, a love song, plaintive and sad, but beautiful.

Slocum found his way to her bed easily for he had retrieved his sack from it after they had come back from the stables. But he could see her there, lying atop the coverlet with the curtains flowing like silken ghosts from the open windows nearby. The lamp bathed her body in a golden glow and he thought she looked like some Egyptian princess, one leg folded over the other, slightly cocked to reveal the clean lines from ankle to hip.

"You can take off those shorts, John," she said. "I didn't know you were modest."

"Well, one never knows what to expect when invited to a lady's room. I thought maybe you were modest."

"In the daytime, I am," she said.

Slocum took off his shorts and slid onto the bed next to her. She smelled of lilacs and sage as she opened her arms in anticipation. Slocum slid closer, and she embraced him, wrapping her arms around him and mashing him against her breasts.

"It feels good to have a man in my bed," she said. "Again."

"Again?"

"I had a beau once, John. I was very fond of him. We were to be married, and he begged me for a taste before our wedding day."

"And you took him to your bed?"

"Yes. I was young. I had no experience."

"That's how you gain experience, Bettilee."

"I know, but it was a bad one. He-he died in my arms. Before . . . before anything happened."

"He died in your bed? What happened?"

"The doctor said he had a rheumatic heart. The excitement was too great for poor Todd."

"It must be a painful memory for you," Slocum said.

She kissed him then and squeezed him tightly. "It was," she said, "until now. As I said, I was very young. I hardly remember Todd, or even what he looked like."

"I'm sorry, Bettilee."

"I didn't mean to bring it up now, but I just wanted you to know that there has been no one since Todd."

"Why?"

"I-I was afraid. I never had the desire, I guess. Todd

was a weakling. Not just from the rheumatic fever he had as a boy, but a weakling. I told myself that if I ever took a man to my bed again, it would be someone strong. Like you."

Slocum returned her kiss and placed a hand on her breast. It was full and plump and soft. "I'm glad you did," he said. "Took me to your bed, that is."

"Make me a woman, John. Please. I've longed for this moment. I've ached inside to be with a good, strong man."

Slocum let his hands roam all over her luscious body. She writhed and squirmed under the touch of his deft fingers on her belly, her legs, along every curve and crevice of her naked body. He plied her wiry nest and slid a finger inside her. She became wet and juicy quickly and her hips rose and fell with the rhythm of his gentle stroking.

"Oh, John, that feels so good," she said. "I'm all wet inside. I'm ready."

"Yes," he husked and mounted her. She spread her legs, and he descended atop her, burying his rigid shaft in her cunt. He felt the leathery resistance of her maidenhead and weakened it with repeated thrusts of his swollen cock. She moaned softly and her fingers dug into his bare back as the intensity of the experience gripped her, held her fast in its lustful vice.

"Now," she said. "Break it. I want you in me all the way."

Her words made his cock swell even more, and he put more pressure on the hymen that guarded her inner portal. He thrust deep again and again and finally he felt the thin membrane part as he pumped hard against it. He felt a rush of blood and heard her cry out a small scream at the brief pain it brought.

"Yes, yes," she moaned as Slocum slid in all the way, deep into her cunt. He felt her body buck against the shock of it, and then she matched his rhythm with her own. Finally he felt her body quiver as it shook with repeated climaxes.

She let her hands fall from his back as she braced herself on the bed. The slats creaked and the bed rocked with the motion of their lovemaking, and he drove into her steaming cunt harder and harder, faster and faster until she screamed, loudly this time, and her entire body trembled with the spasms of her tumbling climaxes, one after the other, until it was just one searing, electric sensation of pure pleasure.

"Put your seed in me, John. I want to feel it shoot into me."

She grabbed him again, her arms clasping his back. She held on as he slammed into her even harder and faster. Then, in a rush that was like a great river flooding through him, he exploded his balls inside Bettilee and her long scream of pleasure ended in a huge, grateful sigh.

"Oh, John. I never expected it to be so wonderful. This wonderful. I'm so happy."

"I'm glad," he said, draining the last of his seed into her velvety wet cunt. "You gave me much pleasure, too."

"I-I never knew it would be like this," she whispered, as if in a trance. "So grand, so sweet, so wonderful."

"I hope it was worth waiting for, Bettilee."

"Yes, yes, it was. I'm still somewhere up high on a cloud. I feel like I'm floating down very slowly, and I never want to come back to earth."

Slocum chuckled. "I'm right up there with you," he said.

He slid from her body and lay on his back, panting for

breath. She reached over and touched him, touched the limp cock and rubbed its wetness onto her palm.

"I could just lie here next to you forever, John."

"In a while," he said. "I'll want you again."

"I want you back inside me right now. But you're not ready."

"It won't be long, if you keep your hand where it is."

"You amaze me," she said. "I'm just amazed."

She sighed deeply and continued to knead his cock, caressing it with her fingers and squeezing it in all the right places.

It wasn't long before she made him ready again. And he took her to even greater heights, rising with her to a mountain of pleasure where they both floated in a haze of wonder and joy as if they had made love for the first time.

Much later, John lit a cheroot and put on his shorts. Bettilee turned the wick up on the lamp and she opened the locket her brother Ben had given to Slocum.

"I'll get the map halves," she said, speaking as if still in a trance. While she did that, Slocum examined the overlays that had been in the locket. They were on very thin onionskin paper and were just a series of straight and curved lines that made no sense. However he knew they would match up to similar markings on the two halves of the maps made by her father.

Bettilee laid out the two halves of the map her father had painstakingly drawn and pushed them together.

"They match up," she said. "Perfectly."

"Do you know where the mine is?" Slocum asked.

"Not yet. I'm sure he wouldn't mark the exact place on either half of the map. But the overlays might show us where it is."

"Be careful with those overlays," he said.

"Do you know how they work, John? I've never seen such small pieces of paper and so thin like these."

"Let me look at the map, and I'll see if I can find the keys that will tell me where to put the overlays."

Slocum studied the map carefully, turning his head to different angles to look for curves and lines that resembled those on the overlays.

"This is an odd map," Slocum said. "Generally, the overlay would be just one sheet, and you'd be able to see the first map underneath."

"So those little pieces are like a jigsaw puzzle."

"Yeah, but I'm wondering how we can even figure out where that mine is after I find the places for the overlays to mark a clear route to your father's claim."

"Can I help?" she asked.

"No, it's pretty much a one-person job at this point. I've already found a couple of likely places where the overlays should fit. I'll know more when I put them in place."

"Will it take long?" she asked.

"I don't know," Slocum said.

Then he began to play with one of the overlays on the map. That one connected other lines Bettilee's father had drawn. Slocum smacked his lips in satisfaction. He carefully placed another overlay a short distance from the first one and then another.

Slowly, the map started to take on a different complexion. The overlays bridged gaps in the original map and connected roads and pathways through the mountains to the west of Taos.

But the chore became more difficult as the overlays became more intricate and less simple than the ones he had already laid down. It seemed to him that neither he nor Bettilee were breathing, as if they were both afraid they might blow the overlays already set down, clear off the map.

"Wait a minute," Slocum said, after another close examination of the map. "Who tore this map in two when your father gave you the one half?"

"Why, he did, John. Why?"

Slocum carefully pushed the two halves of the map even closer together, then bent over to study it.

"Aha," he said. "He tore the map right along a river or a creek. That's the key."

"Why, yes, there is a creek up that way. My father used to take us up there. When he was still looking around. I recognize it now."

"And this last piece . . . I was looking for a mark that could make an $X$ on the map, but now I see it."

Slocum laid the last overlay down near the top of the tear that represented the creek. It fit a little bit to the left of the creek line.

Then he straightened up and they both looked at that last clue Ethan Travers had left behind.

"It's a cross," Slocum said. "Not an $X$. And that's where your father's mine is. Of course, it doesn't say how far from the creek the cross is or the mine. It could be a mile or ten miles. The map has no scale."

"Oh, my heavens," Bettilee explained. "That explains everything."

"What do you mean?" Slocum asked.

"Just a minute," she said and began digging in her carpetbag. She produced a folded piece of paper. She opened it and read it quickly. "My father gave me this and said to keep it. He said it would make sense some day."

"What is it, Bettilee?"

"He wrote: 'When you have joined the two halves together and solved the puzzle, then it's fifty yards from the creek to the cross.' I never knew what he meant until now."

"So, that's it," Slocum said. "That's the last piece in place. Now you know where the mine is. Do you think you can find it?"

She came close to him and put an arm over his shoulder.

"John, we'll find it together. I think my father would have wanted it that way."

"Are you sure?" he asked.

"Yes," she said. "I'm very sure. We'll ride out there tomorrow, after I see Ben. Oh, he'll be so happy."

Slocum said nothing. He just hoped that Ben would be alive when they went to the clinic in the morning. And he had another concern that was even more weighty than that one.

There was still the Dunbars and their crony to consider. If they had any idea of where that silver mine was, they would surely be waiting for them to show up somewhere along that creek.

But Slocum said nothing to Bettilee.

He didn't want to spoil her happiness. Not this night, this very special night.

# 21

The screams froze the blood in Bettilee's veins as she entered the Aguirre clinic. Slocum, right behind her, had to step in and put his arm around her waist and lead her inside. The hackles rose on the back of his neck.

"It's Ben," Bettilee exclaimed.

"Wait here. I'll go see what's going on," Slocum said.

"No-no, I want to go with you. My God, what's that doctor doing to him?"

Slocum had a pretty good idea, but he didn't tell Bettilee. He released his hold on her and charged through the door of the waiting room, leaving her behind. He stalked into the operating room where Dr. Aguirre was standing over Ben's naked leg. Two nurses held Ben down. There was blood all over the doctor's apron and on the floor and the operating table.

Aguirre looked up when Slocum entered the room. The shelves on two walls were lined with lanterns, their wicks turned up high, mirrors behind them to reflect light on the operating table. Near the other side of the room, nearest to where Aguirre stood, there was a small *horno*, an adobe stove in the shape of a beehive. The stove was blazing with burning wood and there were pokers shoved inside and resting on the coals.

"You can help, Slocum," Aguirre said. "Hold this young man down while I finish sawing off his leg."

Ben screamed again and struggled to rise from the table. The nurses, their faces glistening with sweat, pushed downward on Ben's arms. The veins in the nurses' necks stood out in relief, and the muscles in their small arms quivered from the strain.

Slocum ran to the table, leaned his rifle against the wall and took over for one of the nurses, pushing her aside. She muttered her thanks in Spanish and sighed as she collapsed against the back wall.

"Almost finished," Aguirre said.

"Did you have to take the leg?" Slocum asked.

"Either that, or young Ben here would be dead before another sunset."

Bettilee entered the room and rushed to stand next to the other nurse, on the near side of the table. She looked at Ben's face, which was contorted in agony.

"Oh, Ben," she said. "I'm so sorry."

"Help hold your brother down, Miss Travers," Aguirre said. "I am sorry he is in so much pain. But it cannot be helped."

Dr. Aguirre bore down on the saw and cut through the bone. Ben's leg fell to the floor with a thump. Blood spurted from the raw stump.

Aguirre set the saw down quickly and turned to the small stove. He grabbed a pair of towels from the foot of Ben's table and grabbed two of the pokers. The ends were glowing a cherry red.

Ben screamed and then lapsed into unconsciousness. Bettilee gripped her brother's arm as if to hold on so that if she fainted she would not fall.

Aguirre touched the stump of Ben's leg with the ends of both pokers, deftly cauterizing the exposed veins, turning the pokers in his hands like a magician so that the heat seared the wound in the most crucial places. The smell of burning flesh filled the room. Slocum fought back the gagging in his throat, and he heard Bettilee retch until she brought her heaving stomach under control.

"It is almost over," Aguirre said, putting the pokers back into the fire, and drawing a third hot poker from the flames and coals. He finished cauterizing the wound and then called to the nurse to bring bandages and salve.

"He is asleep now," Aguirre said. "But he will awaken to much pain. I can help him with that a little."

"Is he going to live?" Bettilee asked, her voice quavering with emotion.

"Yes, I think this will stop the infection. Whoever kept him alive and first cauterized his wound did a goodness to Ben that made him live this long."

"That was Mr. Slocum," Bettilee said, gulping in air when she finished. Slocum looked at her, saw that the color had drained from her face. She looked as if she were going to be sick, but he could see that she was fighting not to vomit.

"Then you should thank Mr. Slocum for saving the life of your brother. I am still in wonderment that Ben was able to live this long. There was much infection and there is yet much. He is not well yet, but we will care for him, and he will learn to walk with crutches. Or there are artisans in Taos who can carve for him a wooden leg."

"I'm grateful to you, Dr. Aguirre." She stared at Ben's

sweat-oiled face and stroked his forehead. "He lo-looks so sad and weak. Is there anything I can do to make him feel better?"

"It would be better if you did not try to help. I have performed these amputations before. I know the questions he will ask, and I know the fears he will have. You should return in a week and see how he acts now that he has lost one of his legs."

"A week?"

"He will not be very strong, and I wish to keep him calm. The wound must not break open. I will have to do some sewing when the wound has healed a little more."

"I see," Bettilee said, but Slocum could see that she was very upset. Still, he could see the wisdom of Dr. Aguirre's words. He was the professional here, not he or Bettilee.

The nurse brought the doctor new bandages and a tin of salve. Then she started shooing Slocum and Bettilee from the room. Slocum walked over and retrieved his rifle, which he had leaned against the wall.

"Yes, you must go, Miss Travers and Mr. Slocum. Come back in a week. But first there is the matter of my bill for last night on your two friends."

"What?" Bettilee said.

"They woke me up, and I had to tend to their injuries. They were mostly minor. They said that you would pay me when you came here this morning."

"I don't know what you're talking about, Dr. Aguirre."

"I do," Slocum said to her. Then, to Aguirre, he said: "What were the names of these two friends, Doctor?"

"Mr. Rand and Mr. Sutphen. The cost is three dollars American money for my services."

"Those are not friends of mine, Doctor," Bettilee protested. "Why, they tried to kill us last night. Where do you think they got their injuries?"

"Ah, they did not tell me. But since I smelled the liquor on the breath of the men, I thought that perhaps they had gotten hurt while fighting in one of our cantinas."

"They stole my wagon, and Mr. Slocum stopped them. He was the one who fought with them. And he is the one who beat them soundly, Doctor."

Aguirre smiled.

"Then, it is my mistake. I believed the men when they told me you would pay for my services."

Slocum reached into his pocket. He drew out some paper money and peeled off three one-dollar bills. He handed them to the nurse.

"I will pay their bill, Doctor," Slocum said. "In a way, I feel responsible."

"That is very kind of you, Mr. Slocum. You are a good man."

"I wouldn't pay their damned bill," Bettilee said. "The nerve of those two ruffians. What nerve."

Slocum put his arm around Bettilee. "Calm down, Bettilee. I don't mind paying. It gives me a kind of small pleasure, in fact."

"Oh, you," she said and stormed from the room.

Slocum looked at Aguirre and shrugged.

"Women," Aguirre said. "They can be a puzzle, no?"

"I will probably never understand them, Doctor. Thanks. Thanks for taking care of Ben. We'll be seeing you. Do you want me to pay you for what you've done with him so far?"

Aguirre shook his head. "No, that will not be necessary. I trust you, Mr. Slocum. And there are few men that I can say that about."

"Well, thanks, Doctor. We'll see you in a week."

"*Vaya con Dios*," the doctor said, then turned back to his bandaging of Ben's amputated leg.

Slocum left the office to find Bettilee outside, still fuming.

"Oh, those two rascals," she said. "I could just choke them both."

"Easy, Bettilee. No harm done. Your brother is in good hands, and we have some riding to do."

"Yes, you're right. I think I'm taking my anger out on those two thieves because I feel so helpless. I can't do anything for my brother. I can only wait and worry."

"You can wait," he said, "but worrying won't help anyone, least of all him."

"You're right, of course. I'm grateful to have you by my side through all this."

"My pleasure, Bettilee. Now, do you think you can follow that map of your father's?"

"Yes, I know I can. I know most of it by heart. And I have a pretty good idea about the parts I'm not familiar with."

Slocum was riding the black he had rented in Pueblo, and Bettilee had ridden one of the horses from the wagon team. And as he had observed, she was a good rider. She was dressed in a riding outfit and boots. And she wore her pistol on her hip, concealed by a shawl she had over her shoulders.

"Shall we start out then?" he asked.

"I'm glad we had the inn pack us a lunch and some extra food in case we have to stay up there overnight. And I trust your bedroll is big enough for both of us."

"It is," Slocum said, "and that, too, would be my pleasure."

"What? To take me to your bed?"

"To my bedroll. Yes'm."

Slocum grinned and Bettilee rewarded him with a peck on his cheek.

They crossed the street and mounted up. The sun was just clearing the horizon as they set out from Taos, lighting the Sangre de Cristo range with its snowy peaks glistening a brilliant white against the blue of the sky.

# 22

Bettilee led them to the place where the little creek emptied into the Rio Grande. The road there was well rutted and showed signs of heavy use. More ominous, Slocum found fresh horse tracks, three separate and distinct tracks, leading away from Taos. He knew that Bettilee had not noticed them, or if she had, the importance of them had not registered strongly enough for her to comment on them.

The tracks were faint, as if the wind had blown over them since they were made, but Slocum figured they were no more than two days old.

"Was this road here when your father first came up this way?" Slocum asked.

"Yes," Bettilee replied. "Father told us it was an old woodcutters road. As you can see, there are a lot of trees that have been cut down."

"But there's also new growth. So, this must be a very old road."

"I think it is. Our father called this creek Rio Plata,

*Silver Creek.* He named it even before he discovered silver up in the mountains."

"Was your father a geologist?"

"He read books about geology, studied rocks and such. On his own."

"Did he know he'd find silver higher up?"

"He said that's why he named this Silver Creek. He thought it would bring him good luck. He said there should be silver, and perhaps gold, somewhere up there."

She looked up at the range of mountains and breathed deep of the clear fresh air. They rode side by side, and the creek was just as it had been drawn on the map. It ran straight and true with no large bends and the sunlight made it glisten and sparkle as it flowed eastward into the Rio Grande.

When they stopped so that both Bettilee and Slocum could relieve themselves, it was midmorning and they had made fair time. The horses were used to the mountains and did not overexert themselves, but kept a steady pace.

Slocum lit a cheroot and studied the horse tracks more closely while Bettilee was off in the pines and aspen that grew thick on both sides of the creek. He noticed the nick in one shoe that he had seen when he first encountered them far to the north.

So, he knew that somewhere up ahead, Dunbar, Ellie, and the third rider were probably waiting in ambush for Bettilee and Slocum to show up. And he knew that it would be suicide to ride up on that open road where they could probably be seen for some distance from where the trio of bushwhackers lay waiting.

Slocum studied the terrain ahead for as far as he could see. He decided that if he and Bettilee kept on their present course they would ride straight into any ambush Dun-

bar had set up. Somehow, he had to be able to come upon
Dunbar and catch him by surprise.

As they were riding, Slocum noticed that there were
trails leading off of the main road along the Rio Plata.
These were strewn with wood chips and dried branches
that had been stripped from downed trees.

When Bettilee returned, Slocum beckoned to her as he
rode off on one such woodcutter's trail.

"Where are you going?" she asked.

"I think that if we stay on this road we're going to be
in trouble. Dunbar and Ellie are somewhere up ahead."

"How do you know, John?"

"They left their tracks."

"Are you sure?"

"Dead sure," Slocum said.

"So what are we going to do?"

"I thought we'd ride through the woods as quiet as we
can, keeping the road and the creek in sight. Then, maybe
we can see Dunbar before he sees us. There's only one
problem, though."

"What's that?" she asked.

"I don't know how far it is to the top of that map where
we start looking for the cross."

Bettilee brightened. She smiled indulgently at Slocum.
Slocum cocked one eye and looked at her as if she had
suddenly gone daft. Then, she smiled.

"Oh, there was something I didn't tell you, John."

"You don't trust me?"

"It slipped my mind, really. Until now."

"Well, now might be a good time to tell me what I
need to know."

She rode over close to Slocum and touched him ten-
derly on the arm. "Of course I trust you, John. I really

did forget. It was something my father told me when he gave me that half of a map."

"And you remember it now?"

"Yes. He said that if I ever needed to find the mine by myself, or with Ben, that I should look for the high blazes on the trees."

"I haven't seen any blazes," Slocum said.

"I know. He said he didn't start them until he was within five miles of where the mine was. He said to count the blazes. At the fifth blaze, I should stop. He said that marked the end of the creek on the map."

"Did he say anything else?"

"No. He said I'd know what that meant when the time came if anything should ever happen to him."

"Which side of the creek are the blazes on? Did he tell you that?"

"He said they would be on my left. He said he stood up in the saddle and cut the blazes with a hatchet so that the elk, bear, and deer wouldn't mark them up."

"Good enough," Slocum said. "We should be getting close to that first blaze then."

"I hope we can see it from here in the woods."

"We'll see, won't we?"

They saw the first blaze clearly after riding another half mile through the woods. Bettilee was following Slocum's instructions. He slowed the horse so they didn't make a lot of noise, and what noise they did make was soaked up by the thick stands of trees they rode through. Slocum was confident that no one on the other side of the creek or up the road could hear them coming.

Slocum saw the second blaze roughly around another mile, he figured, and the third was the same distance. His heart began to beat faster when they saw the fourth blaze.

According to his figuring, they were only a mile away from the fifth blaze. That's when he began wondering if Dunbar had also seen the blazes and realized their importance. There was no mention of them on the half of Travers's map he had in his possession, but Dunbar could easily see that a man didn't mark blazes on trees without a damned good reason, especially blazes that were higher than a man standing on the ground.

Before they reached the fifth blaze, Slocum stretched his arm out behind in a gesture that told Bettilee to stop. At the same time, he reined up his horse. He turned around and put a finger to his lips.

Bettilee reined her horse in and came to a stop. She looked at Slocum, her eyes wide.

Slocum sniffed the air, then beckoned for her to ride up to him, slowly.

"What is it?" she whispered as she came up alongside Slocum.

"I smell smoke," he whispered back. "It's very faint, but I'd bet Dunbar's camp is somewhere up ahead. Maybe around that fifth blaze."

Bettilee sniffed the air and nodded. "I smell it, too. Not fresh smoke. But like smoke that has lingered in the woods after a campfire has been put out."

Slocum nodded, then put his finger to his lips again and gestured for her to stay where she was. He turned his horse around, handed her the reins. He slipped his rifle from its scabbard and stepped down out of the saddle.

When he turned to Bettilee, she opened her mouth as if to speak, but Slocum put his finger to his lips again. Then, he gestured towards the direction he was going to walk and, with his hands, indicated that she should stay where she was. She nodded, showing that she understood.

Slocum had not walked ten paces before he heard a snapping sound off to his right. He ducked and turned to see what had made the sound.

Then, there was an explosion and he heard a horse scream. He whirled to see Bettilee's horse go down, crashing sideways. Suddenly, the woods gave up their silence to the crackling sounds of rifle shots, and he heard bullets whistle through the trees from three directions. He saw Bettilee leap from her horse just before it fell on its side. But she hit the ground hard, and she didn't move after that.

Slocum cocked his rifle. He could not see any of the shooters, but they were working their levers and firing just over his head. He hugged the ground and looked for a big tree to hide behind. He knew he had to get to his feet and start returning fire or they would be overrun in a few minutes. For all he knew Bettilee was shot or knocked out cold.

His heart stopped then.

*She might also be dead.*

He watched his horse turn and trot away toward the creek. A bullet spanged into his saddle, and he saw tufts of leather break free.

Dunbar was trying to kill his horse, and Slocum knew he had to move fast and get into the fight or he'd be at the mercy of three killers who had him outgunned and outnumbered.

He spotted a tree and started crawling toward it.

Then, he heard a shot that was so close he knew he would never make it. Leaves and twigs blew up a few inches from his face.

They had Slocum pinned, and he knew the very next bullet might have his name on it.

# 23

Slocum rolled over twice before the next shot came, a trick he had learned when riding with Quantrill. He wound up close to the tree and on his back, ready to shoot.

The man stepped out from behind a tree, sure of finishing off Slocum. That was a fatal mistake, and he knew it once he put his rifle back to his shoulder. He aimed it at the place where Slocum had been, not where he was now.

Slocum was ready. He didn't even have to shoulder his rifle at that range. He merely lifted the barrel so that his sights rested on the man's chest. As the man swung his rifle toward Slocum, Slocum squeezed the trigger. He saw dust spurt up off the man's grimy shirt, and then he heard a grunt and blood began to spurt from the hole in the man's chest. His rifle slipped from his hands and he crumpled like a scrap of paper in a fire, his legs giving way and his trunk collapsing. He was still gasping for air when he hit the ground, but Slocum knew he was out of commission and dying as his lungs filled up with blood, not air.

It was two against one, now, Slocum thought. But where were Ellie and her father, Jesse? The woods grew quiet for several seconds, then Slocum heard a dry tree branch crack underfoot, followed by a man's voice calling out.

"Luke? Luke, where in hell are you?"

That had to be Dunbar looking for the man Slocum had just shot down. Slocum held his breath and hugged the tree.

"Ellie? Luke over there with you?"

"No, Pa," Ellie replied. "I thought he was over by you."

Loud whispers, so Slocum knew that Ellie and Jesse were not far apart. That made them dangerous. He tried to pinpoint where they were based on the sound of their voices. But he knew the trees could deflect sound and fool a man. Somehow, he knew he had to draw one or both of them out in the open.

Slocum looked over at the man he had shot. He was already dead, or dying. He wished he knew what the man's voice sounded like. If he had heard him speak, he might be able to imitate him.

Slocum then glanced over to where Bettilee had fallen, a few feet behind her horse. To his surprise, she was not there. But he hadn't heard her get up or move around. Did Ellie or her father have Bettilee? Their voices had come from somewhere in that same vicinity, as near as he could figure.

"Damn it, Luke," Dunbar exclaimed.

"Slocum must have killed him," Ellie called out, and this time Slocum knew exactly where both she and her father were. He slid around the tree to put it at his back while he thought it all out. He took a deep breath.

Then, he knew it was worth a try. "Over hear, Jess," Slocum called, holding a hand over his mouth to muffle his voice. He was hoping that Dunbar and Ellie would fall for the trick.

"Luke, damn it, where's Slocum?" Dunbar yelled.

"I got him," Slocum hollered.

"Ellie, he got Slocum."

"That isn't Luke, Pa."

Slocum cursed silently. He gave Ellie credit for being a little smarter than her father.

"It ain't?" Dunbar called out.

"That was Slocum," Ellie shouted. "He probably shot Luke dead."

"Damn." Dunbar believed his daughter, Slocum was sure. "Where's Slocum? Where in hell is Bettilee?"

Slocum had both Dunbars located in his mind. But he was pinned behind a pine tree and there was too much open space around it. If he stepped out, he was liable to be shot by either Ellie or Jesse, or both. The two were situated so that he would be caught in a merciless cross fire.

Slocum waited, his mind working at a swift pace. He had been involved in such standoffs before. As a sniper at Gettysburg, he had learned patience when his nerves were jangling like broken shutters in a windstorm.

But this one was different. He had no idea where Bettilee was. But neither did the Dunbars. And he now knew, they also did not know his position. Which gave him a slight advantage.

Slocum listened for any sound that might show that the Dunbars had run out of patience. The woods deepened with a silence that he could almost touch. It was like that long quiet moment before a battle when both sides were girding for a fight and no one made a sound, each man with his own thoughts of death or of killing, moments when life hung on the brink of eternity and a man faced his deepest fears, or sought for that elusive bolt of courage that would carry him into the fray without fear choking him into a helpless target.

Then, after several long moments, he heard something that sent shivers up his spine and caused the hackles on the back of his neck to stiffen into hard bristles. He felt as if a spider were walking across the back of his neck preparing to bite him at any moment.

The sound he heard was a pistol cocking. And it was so loud in that silence that it seemed like it was right inside his ear. He was sure the Dunbars had heard it, too, and he knew it had not come from either of them.

It had to be Bettilee, Slocum thought.

"What was that?" Jesse Dunbar asked in a single burst of breath. "Ellie?"

Slocum knew, in that moment, that Dunbar was distracted and that this might be his only chance to get out from behind the tree that concealed him. Without further thought, Slocum made a dash to another tree some twenty yards closer to where he had last heard Jesse Dunbar's voice. He ran and fired off a shot in the direction of where he hoped Dunbar still was.

Slocum fired his rifle again then levered another shell into the chamber on the run. He heard the bullet whistle through the woods and smack into a tree. Out of the corner of his eye, he saw Dunbar duck. At the same time, he knew Dunbar had seen him, too.

Dunbar raised his rifle and came out of his crouch. Slocum threw himself headlong on the ground, five feet from the tree he was running toward. Dunbar cracked off a shot that whistled over Slocum's head.

Slocum got a bead on Dunbar and squeezed the trigger, using his elbows for a bipod to steady his aim. Smoke and flame belched from the muzzle of his Winchester, and he saw Dunbar stiffen as a tiny puff of dust sprouted from his shirt.

The shot was high, Slocum thought, but it had struck Dunbar just below his right shoulder, perhaps nicking his lung. He ejected the spent cartridge and heard the next bullet slide into the chamber. He crawled forward, towards the tree he had been heading for as Dunbar took aim at him again. The man was hurt, but he was not down, and he was not dead.

Now, Slocum knew he had to make sure he wasn't in Ellie's sights. And he had to move fast, or Dunbar would have another shot at him. He rolled to his left, toward a pine that would offer him some protection. A split second after he moved, he heard a shot off to his left and dust kicked up where he had been a scant moment before. Sweat beaded up on Slocum's forehead. He knew he was in a bad spot.

Slocum scooted around the tree like a moving arm on an axis. Two more shots rang out, and he heard them smack into the pine tree where he was. Splinters of bark flew off, but he knew he was out of the line of fire for the moment.

Then, he heard footsteps pounding on the leaves and rocks from where Dunbar had last stood. Slocum raised his head slightly and peered around the trunk of the tree. He saw movement and swung his rifle around for a snap shot.

Dunbar stepped into plain view. Slocum dropped the

front blade sight a hair away from Dunbar and squeezed the trigger. Dunbar met the shot with his next stop, and it tore through both lungs. A heavy grunt escaped his lips as blood sprayed from the exit wound, mottling the leaves on a pair of bushes. Dunbar staggered away from Slocum, mortally wounded. His legs flew out from under him, and he struck the ground with a heavy thud.

"Drop it, Ellie, drop your damned rifle."

Bettilee's voice, from somewhere off to his left. Slocum hugged the pine tree and pulled himself up to a standing position, then turned sideways so that he did not present his silhouette to Ellie.

"Go to hell, Bettilee," Ellie shouted.

As Slocum started to peer around the tree, he heard a shot and then a bullet whistled right next to where his head would have been had he taken a look. Needles of bark stung his forehead as the bullet tore a path less than an inch from his head.

At that moment, Slocum heard a six-gun bark.

Once, twice, three times.

Then, silence.

Slocum did not know who had fired the pistol.

Had it been Ellie?

Or Bettilee?

The shots had not come in his direction. He knew that much.

But that was all he knew, and the seconds dragged out in the terrible silence when life and death teeter on the fulcrum of fate as if two ghosts were sitting on a phantom seesaw on the very edge of eternity.

# 24

Slocum waited for what seemed an interminable length of time, straining his ears to pick up the slightest sound that would tell him what was going on.

Finally, a voice broke the silence.

"John?"

The voice was very faint, slightly muffled. But he recognized it. It was Bettilee's voice, and there was a tremor in it as if she were hurt or scared out of her wits.

"Bettilee," Slocum called. "Are you all right?"

"Come over here, John. Quick."

Slocum hesitated, although his mind was racing. It could be a trick, he thought. Ellie could have Bettilee under her control, could have a gun on her, hoping to draw him into the open and kill him.

"Where are you, Bettilee?"

"Over here," she replied.

"Is Ellie with you?"

"Come quick, John. Please. I-I need your help."

Slocum's blood quickened. Something was wrong. Bettilee didn't sound like herself. She didn't sound as if she was in control. And that could mean that Ellie had the drop on her.

He heard a horse snort. Then another one whickered. Whose horses? Slocum wondered.

A plan began to formulate in Slocum's mind. He damned sure wasn't going to just walk out into the open and look for Bettilee. He had a pretty good idea where she was, but sometimes, he reasoned, the short distance between two points was in a roundabout way.

He stepped away from the tree with caution. Then he walked in the opposite direction from where he had placed Bettilee from the sound of her voice. He stepped carefully, avoiding dry twigs and fallen branches. He crept through the woods like a stalking Indian, slow and sure, his rifle at the ready.

Then he made a wide circle and wound up near the road on a direct line with where he had last heard Bettilee's voice. He saw her then, from the back. She was standing straight up, and he thought she might have a pistol in her hand. But he couldn't see her hands at all.

Slocum tiptoed toward Bettilee, holding his Winchester hip-high and pointed straight ahead.

"John, where are you?" Bettilee called out. "Are you coming?"

Slocum came within twenty yards of Bettilee and that's when he saw Ellie, about fifteen feet in front of Bettilee. Ellie was unarmed, or so it seemed, and she was leaning against a tree, bracing it with her back. Ellie looked wan and haggard and utterly defeated.

"Bettilee," Slocum said softly, trying not to startle her.

Bettilee whirled and looked at Slocum, her face stricken with surprise.

"John. You scared me. Come here, quick."

"Is anything wrong, Bettilee?"

She didn't answer as Slocum walked up to her. She had turned back to face Ellie, who had not moved. As Slocum came up beside Bettilee, he saw that Ellie had been hit. She was bleeding from her side.

"You shot Ellie?" he asked.

"Yes," Bettilee replied. "But that's not all. Look."

Bettilee raised her arm and pointed off to her left. Slocum saw two horses standing hipshot in the shade of a copse of trees. But he saw something else, too.

"See?" Bettilee said. "John, I'm shaking inside. I-I've never killed anyone before."

"You bitch," Ellie said. "You oughta be shaking. Slocum, where's my pa, you bastard?"

"I imagine he's in hell," Slocum said. "Or well on his way."

"Bastard," Ellie said and crumpled against the tree until she was in a squatting position.

"John," Bettilee whispered, "I-I feel faint. All this has been very disturbing. I shot those men, and I think they're both dead."

"Who are they?"

"Cleve and that Bob Rand. They must have followed us here."

"That was you shooting the pistol?"

Bettilee nodded. "I didn't think. When I saw them, I just started shooting. They said they'd kill me if I didn't take them to the mine."

"Are you sure they're dead?" Slocum asked.

Bettilee shook her head. "I'm not sure. They both fell down, and then Ellie came after me, and I shot her. It all happened so fast."

Slocum looked at Bettilee in wonderment. "You're quite a shot," he said.

"My father told me that if I ever had to shoot anyone to just do it. He told me not to think about it. He said that once I drew my pistol and cocked it, then I had to go ahead and shoot or someone would kill me."

"Your father gave you good advice."

Out of the corner of his eye, Slocum saw movement from one of the men Bettilee had shot. Cleve Sutphen rose up, and he had a pistol in his hand. Before he could step around Bettilee, she whirled and pointed her pistol at Sutphen. Before Slocum knew what happened, she fired a single shot at Sutphen.

Sutphen looked surprised when the bullet struck him in the middle of his chest. He seemed to hold his breath for a second, then closed his eyes and fell backwards, blood spurting from his chest like a crimson fountain.

Then Ellie came to life. She slipped a hand into her waistband and pulled out a small pistol. Slocum saw it and so did Bettilee.

"I took a page out of your book, Slocum," Ellie said. "I bought myself a hideout pistol. Now, drop those guns or I'll shoot you and Bettilee dead."

Slocum knew she had the drop on him. He started to drop his rifle when Bettilee spun back towards Ellie, swinging her pistol. Slocum saw it bark in her hand. He didn't even know if she had aimed it, but when he looked over at Ellie, she was staggering toward them, blood streaming from her neck. She opened her mouth, but no sound came out. She dropped the small caliber pistol and pitched forward, hitting the ground with a soft thud. She did not move, and Slocum knew she was dead.

"That was my last shot," Bettilee said. "I only keep five bullets in my pistol. For safety's sake."

"Bettilee, I don't think you're going to need another bullet today."

She turned to him and, as the tears started down her cheeks, she embraced Slocum in a grateful hug. She slipped her empty pistol back in its holster and put her other arm around him, squeezing with all her might.

Slocum patted the back of her head.

"It's all over, Bettilee. Now we can go and find that mine your father left you."

She turned her head and kissed him on the cheek.

"I just want to get away from this place. My God, I killed my own half sister."

"Who was going to kill you. She was going to kill both of us."

"Do you know how I was able to do it?" she asked, catching Slocum by surprise.

"Why, I suppose it was because you thought she was going to shoot you."

"Yes, but I kept thinking of my father. And Ellie taunted me about him before you came up, before I shot her the first time."

"Taunted you? About what?"

"She said she killed my father."

"I know she did."

"And she said she enjoyed it."

Bettilee shivered in Slocum's arms, then began sobbing uncontrollably.

"She was deadly," Slocum said. "As deadly as any damsel I ever met."

But, he thought, as he led Bettilee away from that place of death, it appeared Ellie had finally met her match. But

Ellie would kill no more, and the world would be a better place with her absent from it.

Slocum and Bettilee caught up two of the stray horses and began riding toward the silver mine. When she saw the cross, Bettilee seemed to relax, but she began crying again when they found the mine, deep in a cluster of brush, a hole blasted through the rock of a hidden bluff.

She wept because of the sign she saw outside proclaiming the name of the mine.

It read simply: THE BETTILEE MINE.

Watch for

**DANCER'S TRAIL**

295th novel in the exciting SLOCUM series
from Jove

*Coming in September!*

**Explore the exciting Old West with one of the men who made it wild!**